I0586976

Aalia's Guardian Angel

Tahirih Lemon

Cover Design by Unique Designs REM

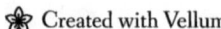 Created with Vellum

Chapter One

Aalia, gasping to breathe, scrambles up onto the cold wet floor of the cave. Frantically wiping clumps of her long black hair from her face, she scans wide-eyed into the depths of the clear bioluminescent blue pool. She's searching for signs of the hideous creature which just seconds ago, had tried to devour her. It had tentacles covered in hundreds of mouths complete with sharp teeth.

Aalia pulls her knees up to her chest and wraps her lanky arms tightly around them in a futile attempt to create some warmth. Her anxiety increases as she notes sharp burning pain radiating from her upper arms. There are tiny tears in her long sleeves and, after rolling them up, she sees multiple bite marks on each arm, where a tentacle had held her in a vicelike grip. Trying not to panic she sucks in a deep, shuddering breath and pulls at her skin with trembling fingers.

Had it injected her with poison? Would the bites become infected?

The large pool is the only source of light in the cave,

casting an eerily faint blue light onto the walls, revealing crevices, cracks and tunnels leading to pitch blackness. She heard faint scratching and scuttling noises in the dark shadows. Heart racing, Aalia peers about, looking for signs of life.

Probably rats or cockroaches.

She pleads, 'God, please do not let there be any snakes.'

Aalia, whispers a voice. *Aalia, my dear.* Confused, she glances around the cave, searching for the source of the gentle, and loving voice. *You are not alone. You have never been alone.*

Trying to ground herself, to remain calm and present in her body, she breathes slow, deep breaths, in and out. She realises the voice came from within her head, but it isn't her mind speaking. Whoever is speaking to her, is using telepathy.

The brief message brings some comfort to her. This is not the first time she has heard voices in her head that are clearly not hers. They are distinct and separate from the negative talk she often experiences when courage is required to try something new, take a risk or stand up against an injustice, when her doubts flood in, trying to dissuade her from acting.

Could this be my guardian angel? she wonders.

A bright light appears deep within one of the tunnels. Aalia stands up and does a quick body check to make sure everything is intact. She has sustained no other injuries. She cautiously enters the luminous tunnel, curious as to its source. *Could be trickery,* warns her ego. *Could be assistance and guidance,* she pushes back.

Relying on her intuition and what she hopes was the recent message of reassurance from her guardian angel, Aalia overrides her ego. She knows it uses fear to paralyse her and to create confusion and indecisiveness. She stops in the middle of a large cavern, directly beneath the dazzling white light of a chandelier-shaped stalactite. Bathed in the light's warmth and love, she feels her determination and courage growing.

All the answers you seek, Aalia, are within you. Seek and you shall find, commands the voice.

She stirs opening her eyes. 'Well, that was very cryptic,' she mutters, staring up at the bedroom ceiling.

Chapter Two

Six Months Earlier

Sorrow envelopes Aalia as she stares at the coffin at the front of the chapel. It's hard to look at the framed photo of her best friend, Charlotte, grinning from ear to ear, which sits on top. She focuses instead on the huge flower arrangement bright with Charlotte's favourite sunflowers. As corny as it sounded, she always thought Charlotte was like a sunflower to all those who met her. She was one of those people whose exuberance for life was contagious.

She feels a stab of anger at the drugged driver, doped up to his eyeballs, who'd hit and killed Charlotte as she walked across a pedestrian crossing on the way to soccer training last Thursday afternoon.

Attempting to wipe away the tears streaming down her face, she resorts to using her sleeves, as her tissues have already disintegrated.

She looks to the front row of seats where Charlotte's parents and younger brother, Liam, are sitting, dressed surprisingly not in black, but bright cheerful colours. Her mother, Mrs Davis, clasps a large sunflower in her hand. Mr Davis peers out a window at an eastern yellow robin perched outside on a fence post, as if looking for a sign. Aalia swallows against the sudden lump in her throat. That was Charlotte's favourite bird. It's unusual to hear its piping call so late in the day. Maybe it's a sign. A sign from Charlotte. A sign from the afterlife.

Liam, leaning against his mother with his head on her shoulder, straightens up and turns. His eyes meet Aalia's briefly. The pain is too great, so she avoids eye contact for the remainder of the funeral.

Her mother squeezes her hand and sweetly smiles with tears forming in her eyes. 'Are you okay?'

Aalia nods and turns faceward to the celebrant. She hardly breathes as she listens, hanging onto every word, trying to visualise images of Charlotte's soul soaring like a bird as described in the reading:

To consider that after the death of the body of the spirit perishes is like imagining that a bird in a cage will be destroyed if the cage is broken, though the bird has nothing to fear from the destruction of the cage. Our body is like the cage, and the spirit is like the bird. We see that without the cage this bird flies in the world of sleep; therefore, if the cage becomes broken, the bird will continue to exist. Its feelings will be even more powerful, its perceptions greater, and its happiness increased. In truth, from hell it reaches a paradise of delights because for the thankful birds there is no paradise greater than freedom from the cage.[1]

. . .

Aalia finds herself staring at the robin outside, still perched in the same spot, instead of characteristically flitting from perch to perch looking for insects to eat. It stands poised with reverence, as if listening, and observing the service alongside the rest of the congregation.

Chapter Three

Later Aalia looks in the mirror to ensure she has removed the smudges of mascara that streaked her face. She slathers on moisturiser, feeling the coolness on her skin, and examines her complexion for imperfections, blackheads, and any white-headed pimples that have sprouted. Her grandmother used to describe her complexion as caramel chocolate ice cream with chocolate sprinkles. When she was younger, she'd loved her grandmother's description, but now at fifteen she hates it; especially the part about chocolate sprinkles, despite being a chocolate lover.

Eyes widening for a moment in disbelief, Aalia jerks from the mirror. Her hazel eyes have transformed into her grandmother's dark brown eyes, staring back at her.

'Grandma is that you?' she whispers.

Her transfigured image smiles back at her, a twinkle in her eyes, before transitioning back into hazel eyes.

'I must be going crazy,' she mutters as she switches off the bathroom light and heads to the loungeroom to wish her parents goodnight.

Still stunned and disoriented, Aalia doesn't mention what she's just witnessed. She knows her parents are worried enough about her mental wellbeing since the death of her best friend, checking with her constantly, looking at her with worried frowns.

'Goodnight, Mum and Dad,' she says giving her mother a hug first.

'Goodnight, Aalia. I know today was very emotional and taxing for you. For all of us. We miss Charlotte too. She was like our second daughter,' says Mum as she embraces her tightly.

Tears start to form and spill over. 'I miss her so much,' sobs Aalia.

'I know you do,' says Mum, rubbing her back. 'Remember, she's always in your heart. She'll live on through your memories, and you have so many good ones to hold onto and cherish.'

Her father gets up from his comfy, worn leather armchair and joins in, creating a family hug, as he kisses the top of her head. 'Remember Charlotte isn't gone forever; she's now in heaven. One day, when it's your time, you'll be together again.'

Too upset to respond, she merely nods, and pulls away before heading to her bedroom.

* * *

Tossing and turning, she glances at the full moon shining through the trees outside her bedroom window, revealed intermittently by the flutter of the sheer curtains.

Aalia wonders if she saw her grandmother in spirit or imagined her. Perhaps her grief over Charlotte's death has opened old wounds, including the unexpected death of her grandmother. She didn't get to say goodbye to her either.

She came home from school one day and saw her mother seated dazed at the dining table in front of a cold cup of tea. When Aalia entered the kitchen her mother slowly looked up with red swollen eyes, as tears streamed down her face. Her father had embraced her tightly. As if time had stood still, she'd listened as he told her that her grandmother had died earlier that morning from an aneurysm. He explained a blood vessel in her brain had burst, and that there was no way of knowing beforehand. It was just her time.

Familiar smells regularly triggered memories of her grandmother's presence. Jasmine was a big one. Her grandmother, who didn't believe in perfume but rather used essential oils, would generously dab herself with jasmine oil most days. The scent of lavender meant she was experiencing insomnia. Sweet orange signalled she was feeling a little bit anxious or stressed about something, but Aalia never knew what.

The smell of apple and cinnamon reminded her of her grandmother's famous apple pie topped with a slice of cheddar cheese. The first time Charlotte had a slice of the pie, she'd been puzzled as to why Aalia's family served it with cheese instead of whipped cream. Reluctantly, she'd tried it, and quickly became a convert.

Her grandmother's house lured in visitors with its aromas of sandalwood and cloves. One was used for polishing the wooden furniture; the other for preventing mould. Aalia was grateful her grandmother hadn't smelled musty and of mothballs like some other old folks.

Resisting heavy and drooping eyelids, she succumbs to sleep.

Chapter Four

Feeling somewhat like a social science experiment, Aalia warmly smiles as Ms Mason, the Year 10 Coordinator, introduces her to Willow, a new student in her cohort. She has been assigned as Willow's buddy to assist her to feel welcome and transition into a new school.

Willow shyly returns the smile, looking up slightly, revealing green eyes from behind her auburn fringe, before returning her gaze to her newly polished black leather shoes, a compulsory part of the school uniform.

'Well, I'll leave you girls to it. I'm sure Aalia will make you feel welcome, as will the other students,' chirps Ms Mason. 'Remember, if you have any concerns, you can always arrange a time to chat. My door's always open.'

'I'm sorry you're stuck being my buddy,' mumbles Willow, when Ms Mason is no longer within hearing range.

'Not at all, I'm happy to. It'd be hard starting at a new high school, making new friends, trying to work out where you fit and who's genuinely your friend,' Aalia responds. 'Sorry, you didn't get paired with a cool, popular student.'

Willow looks directly into her eyes for the first time since their introduction, smiling slightly. 'I was never cool or popular in my previous school.'

'Well, look at that, we already have something in common. What electives have you chosen? I do Visual Arts; Film, Television and News Media; History, and Biology.'

'I'm doing Visual Arts and Film too, so we'll be in those classes together. I'm also doing Business Studies, which my dad recommended, and Japanese because I really want to go to Japan one day. I love watching anime and reading manga novels. Do you?'

'I sometimes watch anime but can't say I'm into reading manga novels. I've never tried,' she admits.

'I'll lend you one of my favourites,' Willow offers. 'You can also watch it in anime.'

'Okay, but I'm more of a dystopia and mystery fan. Maybe we can watch some of the anime from the series instead?' she suggests.

'Sure, I don't mind watching it from the beginning with you one day,' agrees Willow.

'I don't know about you but I'm starving. Did you bring your lunch, or do you want to get something from the canteen?' asks Aalia.

'My dad gave me some money to buy lunch. He always does.' Willow stuck her hands into her pockets.

'You're lucky. I get lunch money once a fortnight. Otherwise, I have to eat whatever healthy lunch my mum prepares,' she complains.

'My mother used to make my lunch.' Willow sighs. 'I miss her cooking. After a while, you get sick of buying lunch every day.'

'Why doesn't your mum cook anymore. Is she away, or sick?'

A shadow of grief washes over Willow's pale face. 'My mum died last year. That's why we moved here. Dad wanted to get away. A new start.'

'I'm...I'm so sorry. My best friend, Charlotte, died earlier this year.' It then dawns on Aalia, why Ms Mason paired them together. They'd both suffered loss. They're both grieving.

* * *

Walking out the school gates after the bell, Aalia turns to Willow. 'Are you walking home?'

'My dad is picking me up today, as it's my first day. I live within walking distance, about twenty minutes.' She points in the direction across and up the hill towards the Red Gum Park. 'Maybe one afternoon you can walk to my house, and we can hang out,' she suggests.

'I'd like that,' Aalia replies. 'But my parents will have to meet you and your dad before they'll let me go to your house. They're strict about knowing where I go and who I hang out with. But I'm sure they'll be happy to see me going to a friend's house after all this time.'

'Okay, sounds good. I see my dad across the road. I better go. See you tomorrow,' Willow says.

'Definitely.' Aalia smiles as she waves before heading to the bus stop; her least favourite time of the day, the long-dreaded bus ride home.

* * *

Staring out the window, engrossed in her own thoughts, Aalia reminisces about how she and Charlotte used to catch the bus home together. Charlotte was well liked. She was one of those people who was friendly and sociable to everyone, regardless of who they were. She was friends with the popular kids, the smart kids, sporty kids, drama and art kids, the skaters, even the emos and goths although she avoided the weird kids on drugs. Aalia, not so much. She was more reserved, and self-conscious. Being one of the tallest girls in school brought unwanted attention. She was still adjusting to her lanky frame and knew she came across as anything but graceful. It was so clichéd that people assumed because she was tall, she'd be good at basketball. Nothing could be farther from the truth.

She was transported back to the present of the noisy bus, reeking of teenage boy sweat and body odour, when someone called her name. She turned in the direction of the familiar voice.

'Hi, Aalia. Are you saving the seat for anyone?' asks Liam, Charlotte's younger brother.

'Um, yes. I mean yes, you can sit here. I'm not saving it for anyone.' She shifts closer to the window, creating more space.

'We haven't seen you at our house for a while,' says Liam. 'We were just talking about it over dinner last night. We miss having you around.'

'I thought it'd be too upsetting and weird if I visited, now that Charlotte is gone. Like a reminder of the past.' Guilt at her self-absorption swamped her; at the fact she hadn't checked on Liam despite the fact that he'd lost his sister; his only sibling.

He shakes his head. 'You're still part of our family. You're like a sister to me. I remember all the pranks you and Charlotte used to play on me.' He smiles.

Her eyes prickle with the start of tears; chest constricting. 'The truth is I think I'd find it awkward. I wouldn't know what to even say to your parents. I can't remember a time when I visited in the past and Charlotte wasn't home.' Aalia feels a little lighter being able to say the words.

He glances down and then back to her; she notices his jaw clench. 'Can I ask you something?'

'Sure.' Her curiosity is piqued.

'This may sound weird. But do you sometimes feel as if Charlotte's around you? Or have you had dreams about her?'

Sitting in stunned silence, unsure of how to respond, she hesitates before answering. 'I sometimes feel like Charlotte is around me. I'm not sure if I'm imagining it because I miss her so much, or if it's really her. I haven't had a dream about her. I thought I might because I used to have dreams about my grandmother after she died. They felt so real. She seemed so happy and told me not to worry. I sometimes feel her presence too.' Aalia held back her recent experience with the mirror.

He fidgets with the seat in front of them for a moment and she waits for him to talk. 'I have dreams of Charlotte. She talks to me and tells me she loves me.' He takes a deep breath, 'Last night, though, she said to me, "Help Willow." I don't even know a Willow. Does that mean anything to you?'

She felt the colour drain from her face. 'What? What did you say? Willow? Help her? How? How does she know about Willow? I just met her today.'

'Wow, I don't know. That's just what she said.' He grins. 'Talk about moving fast, though.' Aalia can see he's as much in awe of Charlotte's abilities in the afterlife as she is. 'If she tells me anything else, I'll let you know.'

Confused and distracted, Aalia sits in a silent trance looking out at suburbia.

'Well, this is me.' Liam stands up, throwing his backpack over his shoulder, but he hesitates for a moment. 'I miss you. It'd be great if you came over. Mum and Dad would love it.'

She turns, facing him. 'Oh, okay, I'll think about it.'

'Bye, Aalia.'

'See you, Liam.'

Chapter Five

Aalia haphazardly moves the food around her dinner plate, occasionally inspecting before eating each morsel until she is drawn back into the conversation.

'Did something happen at school today that upset you?' asks Mum.

'What? No. I mean not really. I guess so,' she stumbles. 'Liam sat next to me on the school bus. It was weird, unsettling to see him. I haven't seen him, well not up close, or spoken to him since the wake.'

'How are Liam and his parents?' asks Dad.

'Ah, they're okay, I guess. He said they miss me coming to their house and that I should visit one day.'

'That would be nice,' agrees Mum. 'You can take some cut flowers from the garden, and I can bake them a cake. When were you thinking of going? This weekend?'

'Um, yeah. I guess I could go this weekend. I hadn't planned on it, but I could,' responds Aalia.

'Great, just let me know what cake to bake and I'll get the ingredients,' offers Mum.

'Oh, yeah, I just remembered, I met a new girl at school today, Willow. Well Ms. Mason asked me to be her buddy. She seems nice.'

'Why don't you invite her over after school one day? I'm sure she could do with a friend, being new and all,' suggests Dad.

'Sure, okay. I'll ask her,' replies Aalia pushing her chair back. 'Thanks for dinner. Sorry I haven't eaten it all, I guess I'm not very hungry tonight. I have a biology report to work on.'

* * *

Staring blankly at the computer screen opened onto the results section of her biology report, Aalia's mind dissects her earlier conversation with Liam. *Why hasn't Charlotte visited me? I'm supposed to be her best friend. And what's this about helping Willow?*

'Why didn't you ask me yourself?' she blurts. 'Is that all you have to say to your best friend after all this time? *Help Willow.*'

Angry and hurt, she wipes away the tears running down her cheeks. 'So much for being best friends. Well, if you want me to help Willow, I need more details. I don't even know her,' she says aloud, looking around the empty room in case Charlotte is present.

Following several unsuccessful attempts to make headway on her report, she gives up after reading the same paragraph repeatedly. *There's no use, I can't concentrate. I'll look at it tomorrow or on the weekend.*

Instead, she searches the internet for "communicating with the dead". Who knew there were so many ways the dead communicate with their loved ones? Birds! Birds will do something unusual to get your attention. She pauses.

The eastern yellow robin, outside the chapel window. That was Charlotte! She was giving us a sign that she's okay and free like a bird. She smiles, as her anger towards Charlotte subsides. *There may have been other signs, but I didn't recognise them. I'll have to pay closer attention.*

She rummages through her desk drawer looking for the program from Charlotte's funeral. She locates it and says the prayer for the dead.

O my God! O Thou forgiver of sins, bestower of gifts, dispeller of afflictions! Verily, I beseech Thee to forgive the sins of such as have abandoned the physical garment and have ascended to the spiritual world.

O my Lord! Purify them from trespasses, dispel their sorrows, and change their darkness into light. Cause them to enter the garden of happiness, cleanse them with the most pure water, and grant them to behold Thy splendours on the loftiest mount.[2]

Feeling light-hearted, she uses a tissue to wipe away her tears and blow her nose. She feels an inner peace through her pain and struggles to find the words to describe the feeling. It's as if her body is vibrating and overwhelmed by emotions of sorrow and joy simultaneously, spilling over and out of her. At that moment she feels connected to Charlotte as if she is in the room, in spirit.

Exhausted from the mixed emotions, she turns in for the night.

Chapter Six

Waiting out the front of the school gates the next morning, Willow calls out, 'Hi, Aalia.'

'Hi. Have you been waiting long?'

'About half an hour. Dad dropped me off on the way to work. I wasn't sure what time the school buses arrive.'

'My bus is the last one. It drops the students off at Mary Mackillop College first.' Aalia sighs. 'Sometimes we make it just as the bell is ringing and I end up running to get to class on time. Most teachers are cool about it, when we stroll in late because they know about the bus timetable. Except for Mr Reddy, our maths teacher.'

'What does he do when you're late?'

'He gives a lecture about respect and punctuality. He makes you sit in the front and calls on you for your solutions or to work them out on the white board in front of the class.'

'Oh, that isn't good. If your bus is running late, I'll meet you in class because maths is my worst subject,' she confesses. 'Honestly once trigonometry was introduced it all went downhill from there.'

'Well, luckily for you, I'm pretty good at maths. I just

don't like attention drawn to me in class or anytime for that matter.'

The bell rings and students start to scatter in all directions towards the various building blocks.

'We have English this morning, in Block C across the quadrant over there,' points out Aalia. 'We have Mrs O'Sullivan. She makes English fun and interesting.'

As they search for a couple of spare seats in the middle of the classroom towards the window, Paris, a petite blonde student, looks on with curious contempt, and sneers. 'Well, well looks like Aalia found herself another friend. Hey, what's your name?'

'Just ignore her,' whispers Aalia.

'Hey, I'm talking to you, redhead. Are you a mute or something?' She laughs, elbowing her two cheerleaders sitting one on either side. On cue they echo her laugh.

Annoyed, Willow turns around looking directly into Paris' icy blue eyes, and calmly responds, 'Willow. Not that it's any of your business. You're obviously colour blind as my hair is auburn, not red. Go back and crawl under the rock from which you came.'

A few students engrossed in the confrontation sniggered.

'Oh, that wasn't such a good idea. You just made an enemy for life,' Aalia says under her breath.

'Don't you think you're so clever? We'll see about that,' threatens Paris, narrowing her eyes.

'We'll see about what?' asks Mrs O'Sullivan, smiling as she places marked assignments and books onto her desk.

'Nothing, we're just having a chat, welcoming the new girl, Billow. Sorry I mean Pillow. No— that isn't it. Willow. Just remember Weepy Willow.' Paris smiled, tight-lipped.

'Welcome Willow, that's a beautiful name. We are

currently reading a novel. Here's a spare copy for you to borrow,' Mrs O'Sullivan says, handing a book to her.

'Would someone please provide a summary of what has occurred in the book so far?' she asks, optimistically smiling scanning the room for any volunteers.

* * *

'Mmmm, this crunchy chicken burger is so good,' says Willow, appreciatively wiping the juices dribbling down her chin with a napkin. 'You should order this on Friday.'

'Okay, you've convinced me.' Aalia laughs. Biting into her sandwich, she scans the quad for any signs of Paris and her peeps, breathing a sigh of relief. 'Good— no Paris. She's unbearable. You do know you've probably elevated yourself to the rank of her arch enemy.'

'Bring it on. I'm used to girls like her back in Brisbane,' Willow says. 'She'll eventually get tired and bored and move on to another target. People like her are so shallow. I actually pity her.'

'What! Pity her? When she's awful?' Aalia is exasperated.

'She's insufferable, but underneath is a very insecure and unhappy person. Otherwise, why would she go out of her way to bully others? Happy people just don't do things like that.'

'That's true. But I avoid her like the plague,' Aalia states. 'Want to go to library at lunchtime?'

'Okay, but is this an attempt to avoid Paris?'

'Maybe, but, I do need to do some research. Just think of it this way; the more homework we can get done now the less we have to do on the weekend.'

'Well all right. Not normally how I would spend my

lunchtime but today I'll make an exception. I'll see if the library has any manga novels I haven't read.'

'Good idea. By the way, what do you have after lunch?' Aalia asks.

Willow unfolds and studies her class timetable. 'Business Studies and Japanese. I guess that means I won't see you until Monday, then?'

'Probably, we've got family plans this weekend. Would you like to ask your dad if you can come to my house after school on Tuesday? Here's my mobile number.'

'Thanks,' say Willow as she responds to the SMS. 'Now you have mine.'

'Well, I'll see you on Monday. Have a great weekend.'

'Yeah, you too. I'll ask my dad about coming over.'

Chapter Seven

L ater that evening Aalia dreams.

It feels surreal as I walk around my house, from room to room. Although familiar it has an eerie, haunting atmosphere. Unaware at first, I'm following my cat, Abbey, who died a year ago from a brown snake bite. She's walking ahead with a straight up tail.

The whole scene is like a movie being screened with a blue tint. There's no one else in the house. It's as if no one exists but me. As if the house has been vacant for years. I look at family photos hanging on the wall, displayed on the mantelpiece, and notice dust on the surface of the dining table and kitchen top benches. I go into my bedroom searching for something, but I don't know what.

I discover everything in my bedroom is wet. The window had been left open during a storm which had soaked my bedlinen, blankets, and books. To make matters worse, the roof is leaking. I look up and watch water pouring in from the collapsed ceiling. I drop to my knees crying and yelling out of sheer frustration. As I'm dreaming my mouth opens wide, my jaw moving back and forth as I silently wail.

It's the movement of Aalia's jaws wailing that wakes her up. She turns to her side, wiping away the tears with her sheet, noticing the dampness of her pillow where tears had streamed down her face, and the hoarseness of her throat. *What does this dream mean?*

* * *

'Are you ready?' Mum is holding the Devil's chocolate cake standing at the bottom of Mr and Mrs Davis' driveway.

'Yeah, I guess so,' responds Aalia apprehensively as she takes a step towards the front porch. Clutching a bouquet of cut flowers from their garden, she feels her stomach knot as the doorbell rings.

The front door swings open and she steps back, almost losing her balance when Fudge lunges forward desperately trying to greet her, until he's pulled back inside the doorframe.

'Sorry, he's very excited to see you,' apologies Liam grasping the chocolate brown Labrador's collar. He calls out, 'Mum, Mrs Carter, and Aalia are here!'

Stepping aside away from the door clearing the way, he says, 'Come in, Mum's in the kitchen. Dad's at the shops, but he should be back soon. That cake looks delicious. Thank you.'

'What a nice surprise! What beautiful flowers. Are they

from your garden?' asks Mrs Davis as she warmly embraces Aalia.

'Yes, I picked them this morning.'

'That cake looks amazing. So much for trying to reduce my sugar intake. Thank you. It's wonderful seeing you both after so long.' She hugs Aalia's mother. 'Please sit down. I was about to turn on the kettle.'

'Actually, can Aalia and I have a piece of that yummy cake, and eat it out on the deck?' asks Liam.

'What a lovely idea. I'll bring a couple of slices out and something to drink.'

Sitting out on the deck glancing at Aalia sideways, grinning, he admits, 'I'm glad you and your mum came over. It's nice. Like old times. Well not really, but you know what I mean.'

'I do.' She pats the top of Fudge's head, and he drops a ball at her feet. 'I see someone wants to play.'

'He misses Charlotte. She was always his favourite. He often sits outside her door when it's closed, and any chance he gets to sneak inside he'll lie on her bed. It's as if he's waiting for her to return.' He turns away as his eyes start to glisten.

'Here's your cake, and a glass of water,' says Mrs Davis, handing them each a plate and glass. She laughs as Fudge promptly sits down politely. 'No cake for you Fudge. But I did bring you a treat too.' She gives it to him before returning inside.

'By the way, any further clues about the new girl Willow?' Liam asks with a mouthful of cake.

'Ah, no. I'm not sure how Willow needs help. I'm still getting to know her. Maybe it's about something that hasn't happened yet,' she suggests.

'Hmm, could be. I guess we'll have to wait and find out.'

'All I know is she and her dad moved here for a change when her mother died. It may have something to do with that.'

'Could be. Anyway, I'm glad you guys came. It's been especially hard for Mum since Charlotte died. I overheard her the other day talking to Dad about how her friends don't really visit or call, and when she's at the shops they pretend not to see her.'

'Probably because they don't know what to say or they are afraid of saying the wrong thing, and don't want to upset her.'

'That's true,' he agrees. Staring out at the garden, he discloses, 'To be honest, sometimes I wake up and for a second, I forget she's died. It's still hard to believe.'

They sit together in silence eating their cake and watching Fudge enjoying his chewy treat on the lawn.

The wooden wind chimes hanging from a nearby tree start to produce a melody.

'That's weird,' Liam says. 'There's no wind, but the chimes are moving.'

Aalia straightens her back, placing her plate with a few scattered crumbs on the outdoor table, staring at the wind chimes as the bamboo beats out a tune. Somehow it's familiar but she can't quite identify it. Excitedly, she exclaims, 'It may be a sign from Charlotte! A few nights ago, I did some research about how the dead communicate and one of ways is through wind chimes!'

'That's cool. Charlotte, is that you? Hello, Charlotte,' he calls out, getting up, and approaching the jacaranda. 'She's probably happy you've finally visited.'

The chimes suddenly stop moving.

'Well, I guess she just wanted to let us know she's here. Did you know when birds do unusual things it can also be a sign?' she asks. 'I don't know if you noticed outside the window at the chapel on the fence was an eastern yellow robin.'

'No, I didn't. But I remember she liked its song and its bright yellow belly. She liked anything that was bright yellow,' he reminisces.

'Yeah, yellow was her favourite colour.'

He returns to sit on the outdoor chair, gulping the remainder of his water. A serious expression crosses his face. He confesses, 'I don't want to die yet, but I'm looking forward to hanging out with her again. And my pops. The next world sounds amazing, so much better than this world.'

'How do you know?' she asks, widening her eyes, and raising her eyebrows.

'There's a lot written about the next world in the Bahá'i writings. Of course, we can't really imagine it because we don't have the words to describe it,' he answers.

'How's the next world described?'

'Well for starters,' he says, leaning forward as his face lights up in animation, 'there is an infinite number of worlds. We're on a journey, and this is just the start. The next world is described as a world of lights. And all the answers to things we didn't understand in this life will be revealed.'

'That does sound interesting. How can I learn more about it? Do you have a book I can borrow?'

'We have a few. I'll ask Mum before you go. I'm sure she'll be happy to lend you as many as you like.'

She stands up, collecting the plates and glasses. 'We should probably go in and say hi to your dad. I think I heard his voice.'

'Okay. I'll ask Mum which book to lend you.' He opens

the back sliding door, gesturing with an open arm and inviting her to go in first.

'Hi, Mr Davis,' ventures Aalia.

'Why, hello stranger,' Mr Davis greets her as he opens his arms to offer her a hug.

She walks into his arms for a bear hug.

'Mum, Aalia wanted to know if she could borrow a book on the afterlife,' says Liam.

'Of course, I have several. I'll show you where they're on the bookcase and you can select one or more to borrow for as long as you like.' Mrs Davis leads her to the lounge room where an entire wall is covered with bookcases from the floor to the ceiling, stacked with hundreds of books.

'Here they are, on this shelf. This is one of my favourites,' she says handing Aalia a book.

'Thank you, I'll take this one first and then when I return it, I may borrow another.' She glances at the back cover blurb, and flicks through the pages.

'Oh, before I forget, I'm going to start sorting through Charlotte's belongings and turn the room into a guest room. You're more than welcome to go in and take anything of hers that you'd like to keep as a memento.' Mrs Davis smiles through misty eyes. Dabbing her eyes with a tissue she confesses, 'Sorry, I have my moments. I know she's in a better place and not lost to us, but I miss her terribly.'

Struggling to contain her own emotions, looking down fighting back tears, in a quiet voice Aalia replies, 'That's okay I understand. I don't know if I want to go into her room, but I'd like to have her stuffed otter, Chino, from when we went to the zoo. It was her favourite. If that's okay?' she asks tentatively.

'Of course, I'll get him.'

Returning shortly, Mrs Davis hands Chino to Aalia, and

gently offers, 'I'll keep her other things in boxes and when or if you're up to it you can go through them to see if there's anything else you'd like. I can't quite bring myself to donate her things to charity just yet. I prefer to give them to people who knew her.'

'Thanks,' whispers Aalia as she strokes Chino's head.

'Well, I think we'd better go, it's been lovely seeing you all,' announces Aalia's mother. 'I promise it won't be so long between visits. Perhaps you would like to come over for a BBQ one weekend next month?'

'That would be wonderful.' Mrs Davis accompanies them to the front door. 'We'll look forward to it. Thank you again for the flowers and the delicious cake. I don't think the cake will last long.'

On the car ride home, clasping Chino and gazing out the window, a memory is triggered in Aalia:

'What a cool way to celebrate your thirteenth birthday!' I declare, grinning as I nudge Charlotte with my shoulder, leaning against her as we stroll around the zoo.

'I know, right,' agrees Charlotte. 'Let's see the otters; they're my favourite.'

'They're so cute,' I gush as we hurry towards the otter enclosure.

'Perfect timing, they're about to feed them.'

'They sure stink for such adorable creatures.'

'What a life— floating on your back and using your stomach like a dinner plate,' laughs Charlotte.

'I like how they hold hands floating on their back when they sleep so they don't drift apart and lose each other.'

'When we meet up with my mum and Liam later at the shop on the way out, I'm going to buy myself a stuffed otter to remember this birthday.'

* * *

Later that evening before turning in for the night Aalia rummages through the book and comes across the quote:

Sorrow not, if, in these days and on this earthly plane, things contrary to your wishes have been ordained and manifested by God, for days of blissful joy, of heavenly delight, are assuredly in store for you. Worlds, holy and spiritually glorious, will be unveiled to your eyes. You are destined by Him, in this world and hereafter, to partake of their benefits, to share in their joys, and to obtain a portion of their sustaining grace. To each and every one of them you will, no doubt, attain.[3]

Chapter Eight

'Welcome to my home', announces Aalia, pushing open the front door and revealing a well-lit hallway as the sun streams through from behind and from the glass panel on the side of the door. She drops the keys into a beautiful handmade glass bowl. Bending down to remove her shoes, she explains, 'We don't wear shoes in the house.' She places them on a shoe rack next to a potted plant.

'You have a nice place,' comments Willow looking around the modern black and white kitchen with chequered tiled floors, as Aalia hands her a packet of chocolate cream biscuits and pours them some fruit juice.

Stepping down into another room off the kitchen, placing the glasses onto a coffee table, she invites Willow to sit. 'Sit anywhere. This is my favourite room, the sunroom. It used to be Abbey's favourite spot too.' She pauses, holding back tears, and murmurs, 'She was my cat. She died last year from a snake bite.'

'I'm sorry. That'd be hard— losing your best friend and your cat.'

Aalia composes herself and directs Willow to open the packet of biscuits. 'Help yourself. I once ate a whole packet and felt so sick afterwards. They're hard to resist.'

Willow laughs. 'Don't mind if I do. They're very addictive. At least I can help you finish the packet and remove the temptation.'

'I'm thinking of asking my parents if I can get another kitten. I know I can't replace Abbey, but I miss having a cat.'

'If you do, I'll becoming over to play with it. I love kittens, but unfortunately, my dad is allergic to cats. When I was younger, we had a retriever, Saffron. My parents had her before I was born. We had to put her down when she got old, and she lost control of her back legs. I was ten. After that my mum said she couldn't go through that again, so we didn't get another dog.'

'Do you think your dad would let you have a puppy now? To keep you company when he's at work and you're home alone?' Aalia asks.

'I've thought about it. Just not sure about the timing, as we've just moved here. Maybe for my birthday in November. I'll ask.' She gazes wishfully out the window at the backyard.

'Oh, I've been meaning to ask you,' Aalia says. 'Do you know much about the meaning of dreams?' She helps herself to another biscuit.

'I know a little from what my mum told me. She knew a lot about the different meanings of dreams. Wish she was here so we could ask her.' Willow dabs her eyes. 'Sorry, aren't we downers today.'

Aalia hands her a box of tissues. 'It's been so hard losing my best friend, Charlotte. But I can't imagine anything worse than losing my mum.'

'Yeah, it sucks.' Willow sighs. 'So, tell me about your dream.'

'Umm, I don't know if it's appropriate now. But since you asked. I was walking around my home, but no one else seemed to be living there anymore. Oh, except Abbey, who was leading me around the house.' She recounted her dream.

'Cats are meant to be psychic and represent your intuition. It looks as if Abbey was guiding you. Water represents emotions. You're grieving. That makes sense.'

'It does. Thank you. I was afraid it meant my parents were going to die too, and I'd be all alone,' Aalia says with relief, sitting back in the lounge.

'Since we're talking about dreams and things... Have you ever had experiences where you felt impelled to do something suddenly, but you know it would kill you if you did it?'

'What? What do you mean?' Aalia asks.

'Like for example you're travelling in the car with your parents at a hundred kilometres an hour and you suddenly have this urge to just open the car door and fling yourself out. Or walk straight in front of a moving bus. Or if you're walking in a shopping mall and you climb to the third floor, and you have a strong urge to climb over and jump the glass banisters.'

Shocked and speechless initially, Aalia manages to respond cautiously. 'No. Do you? Where's this coming from?'

'Oh, I'd never act on them. They're just fleeting thoughts. It's as if I'm drawn to dying, but not feeling suicidal, if that makes sense. Plus, I resist doing these things because of the mess, hurt and trauma it would cause those witnessing my death, and my dad,' Willow confesses, glancing sideways.

Concerned, Aalia responds, 'I'm glad to hear that. Do you think you should speak to a counsellor about it?'

'My dad took me to counselling for a while after my mum died. I think it was mainly because he didn't want to talk about it. He still doesn't. It's as if my mum never existed,' Willow says in a quiet, regretful voice, looking down at her clasped hands.

'Let's look on the internet and see what it says,' Aalia suggests, typing onto her mobile: *Why do some people think of doing things that might cause their death?* 'According to the internet, *you may be depressed, experiencing anxiety, worried you or someone will die, or you could be grieving,*' she reads. 'I wouldn't be surprised if you're experiencing all these.'

'Good to know I'm normal for once.'

Narrowing her eyes, Aalia weakly smiles at Willow.

'Do you want to watch the first episode of an anime series I've been watching?'

'Sure, let's see what the rave is all about,' Aalia says, picking up the TV remote, searching the internet.

* * *

'How was your afternoon?' asks Dad.

'Great, we just hung out and watched the first episode of an anime series she's into. I haven't made up my mind if I like it yet. Probably need to watch another two to three episodes to get familiar with the different characters.'

'I see someone also loves chocolate biscuits,' teases Mum with an affectionate smile.

'Sorry we ate the whole packet. You know how it is.

34

After all it's your fault I'm a chocolate addict,' replies Aalia cheekily.

'What, no more chocolate biscuits?' mocks Dad widening his eyes and raising his eyebrows.

'There's another packet hidden in the back of the pantry for emergencies,' Mum confesses, tight-lipped and trying to supress a smile.

'Do you think one weekend Willow could stay the night?'

'Yes. Do you have her father's number so we can introduce ourselves and talk to him, since he wasn't home when I dropped her off?' asks Mum.

'After dinner I'll send her a message and ask for it. Thanks Mum and Dad. Could she stay this weekend?'

'Do we have any plans for this weekend, I don't know of?' asks Mum, turning to Dad, who shrugs. 'Yes, that'd be fine. Make sure you find out if she has any food allergies, and what she likes to eat.'

Quickly swallowing the last mouthful of mashed potatoes, Aalia pushes back from the table, picking up her dishes and grinning from ear to ear. 'Thanks Mum and Dad, you're the best,' she says appreciatively. She hurries to her bedroom to retrieve her mobile.

She sends an SMS: 'Hey, guess what? My parents said you can stay the night this weekend! What's your dad's number so they can talk to him about it?'

A message pings back from Willow. 'Cool, I'll ask.'

* * *

Feeling stoked, Aalia, now tucked in bed, picks up Chino and strokes him, talking quietly to herself. 'Looks like I've made a friend.'

She glances to the book on her bedside table; the one she borrowed from Liam's parents. Curious, she opens the book and wonders, Where are you Charlotte and Grandma?

She opens the book and reads:

How does one look forward to the goal of any journey? With hope and with expectation. It is even so with the end of this earthly journey. In the next world, man will find himself freed from many of the disabilities under which he now suffers. Those who have passed on through death, have a sphere of their own. It is not removed from ours; their work, the work of the Kingdom, is ours; but it is sanctified from what we call 'time and place". Time with us is measured by the sun. Where there is no more sunrise, and no more sunset, that kind of time does not exist for man. Those who have ascended have different attributes from those who are still on earth, yet there is no real separation.[4]

Chapter Nine

Sketching with pastels as she wipes her forehead with the back of her hand, Willows says, smiling, 'I'm really looking forward to this weekend.'

'Me too,' says Aalia as she holds her artwork at arm's length to study. 'I feel this is missing something but I'm not sure. It doesn't look balanced.'

'Mine looks kind of dark and depressing.' Willow sighs. 'Mrs Hogan did say to create a piece representing your inner emotions and relationship with your family.'

'Yes, I feel mine is rather sad-looking. I need to balance it with when I feel happy too, otherwise she may refer us to the school counsellor or worse still call in our parents.'

'That's the last thing I need. I'll add some red. Oh, and some yellow. Otherwise, it might be interpreted look like I'm burning in hell. The yellow can represent glimmers of happiness coming through the cracks from within my heart,' Willow contemplates, studying her piece.

'That's very D&M. Glad to hear there's some happiness shining through. I'd like to think I can take the credit for some of that.' Aalia gently nudges Willow with her elbow.

'I'm not at liberty to say.' She grins.

'I can't say sketching with pastels is my favourite medium. It's so messy and smudges too easily,' Aalia says, wiping her hands for the umpteenth time on an old cloth. 'I'm nearly ready for the fixative spray.'

'Me too. I want to finish this before the bell goes.' Willow gently rubs yellow pastels as the final touch.

'That looks quite spiritual; as if you're glowing like a spirit,' Aalia adds thoughtfully, studying Willow's drawing.

'I'll call it bearing my soul,' Willow declares. 'Let's spray them and then it should be time to go. I like having Visual Arts at the end of the day.'

Aalia smiles and nods in agreement as she hands her the spray.

The bell school bell rings. Doors are flung open as hundreds of students pour out of classrooms, scattering across the school grounds like scavenger ants.

'I better run so I don't miss the school bus. What time is your dad dropping you off to my house tomorrow morning?' Aalia asks.

'No sure. I'll text you tonight.'

'Great, okay. See you tomorrow.' Aalia hurries towards the buses.

* * *

Aalia enters the loungeroom holding a mug of hot chocolate. Her parents are chatting, drinking their cups of tea and occasionally glancing at the TV. She smiles at them innocently and sits down. They turn to acknowledge her presence. In her sweetest voice she asks, 'I was wondering if I could have another kitten? I know I can't replace Abbey, but I miss having a cat. I'll look after her and do everything including cleaning the litter this time. I promise.'

Her mother looks at her father to read his initial reaction. He raises his cup of tea to his lips and returns the look while shrugging.

'To be honest, we were expecting you to ask eventually. We'd discussed getting you a kitten for your birthday or even Christmas. We thought we'd wait until you were ready,' confesses Mum.

Aalia beams. She quickly places her mug on the coffee table and jumps up with excitement, taking turns hugging her parents, being careful not to spill their tea.

'You guys are the best! Thank you. Can we go to the Pet Rescue tomorrow morning?'

'Well, I guess so, but isn't Willow coming over for a sleep over? And what time?' asks Mum.

'How about Willow comes with us? Please?' pleads Aalia, clasping her hands together as if in prayer. 'It would cheer her up too. She loves kittens. She can't have a cat because her dad is allergic. We could play with the kitten when she comes over.'

Following a deep, slow sigh, Mum says, 'Sure, why not. I think Abbey's litter tray, bowls and toys are in a box in the garage, and her cat carrier is in there somewhere. You can look for them tomorrow morning.'

Aalia gulps down the remainder of her hot chocolate. 'Thanks again. I'm going to call Willow and tell her the good news.'

* * *

'This is so exciting,' chirps Willow, linking arms with Aalia as they walk through the Pet Rescue's cattery in the kitten section.

'It is,' she agrees. 'It's hard to decide when there're so many cute ones.' She smiles as she puts her fingers through the welded wire mesh, scratching the top of a black and white kitten's head. 'I want a female. I do like tabbies, but I don't want one that looks like Abbey did. That'd be too weird.'

'Hey, come and look at this one.' Willow beckons with one hand while using the other to play with a light silver white tabby by poking her fingers in and out of the mesh. 'Her name is Sapphire according to the sign.'

Aalia bends down next to her looking into the kitten's large round blue-grey eyes. 'She's beautiful. I'll ask if we can hold her.'

The volunteer opens the cage and gently removes the kitten and places her into Aalia's arms. She coos, as she cradles her in the crook of her arm. She runs her open palm along the back of the kitten's spine, and tenderly tickles Sapphire under her chin. 'Her fur is so soft. Her name is perfect. She's perfect.' Turning, facing her mother, holding the kitten up, she declares gushingly, 'This is the one I want. Sapphire. Isn't she just adorable? How can you resist a face like this?'

'Okay, well let's go do the paperwork and pay for her. We need to buy some kitten food, and a couple of new toys just for her,' says Mum, petting the kitten on the head.

'Really? Thanks, Mum. This is turning out to be one of the best days ever.' With a wide grin, eyes shining, Aalia and Willow follow her mother to the office.

'Look at all these toys. What should I pick? A ball or a

toy mouse with a string tied to a stick?' she asks, holding them up for Willow's opinion.

'Why not both? Your mum said you could get a couple of toys, meaning two.'

'Yes, that's true.' Striding towards her mother, placing them onto the counter. she cheerfully announces, 'These two please.'

'I can't wait to play with her at your house. Some kittens like to play hide-in-seek, or so I've heard.'

'Abbey did. She used to hide under the couch and then jump out and grab you around your ankles, then take off.' Aalia smiles, reminiscing.

'If my dad agrees to let me have a puppy; I wonder if they'll become friends. Some cats and dogs become great friends,' Willow suggests.

'Maybe, but not all cats grow to like dogs,' Aalia cautions. 'Abbey tolerated them if they didn't invade her personal space or try to sniff her butt.'

Peering into the cat carrier, on the drive home, Willow observes, 'Sapphire has had too much excitement. She's fallen asleep.'

'I know you're both excited but it's important to let her get plenty of sleep,' says Mum.

'Oh, we will. She can lie in our laps or next to us while we watch TV or play board games,' reassures Aalia.

Chapter Ten

'Yum, warm fudge brownies with vanilla ice cream.' Willow straightens up wide eyed in her chair as Aalia's mother places a bowl in front of her. 'Wow, this is huge. I should have eaten less lasagne.'

'Thanks Mum, you're the best.' Aalia digs in with a spoon.

'You should come over more often, Willow,' invites Dad. 'We don't get dessert like this every night, mainly for special occasions.'

'Oh, I will, don't you worry.' She wipes any traces of ice cream and brownie crumbs from around her mouth with a napkin.

'Glad you're all enjoying it. If I made dessert every night,' says Mum turning to face Dad, with raised eyebrows, 'we'd become diabetic.'

'Thanks Mrs Carter.' Willow slowly exhales. 'I'm so full. I don't know if I can even walk.'

'Yes, thanks again, Mum,' says Aalia, placing the finger-cleaned bowls into the kitchen sink. She announces, 'We're going to my room to hang out and probably watch some anime.'

'Sounds like fun. Don't stay up too late. Remember to ignore Sapphire when she wakes up mewing in the middle of the night in the laundry. It will take her a while to get used to sleeping on her own,' advises Mum.

'Oh, okay,' sighs Aalia, her shoulders dropping.

'Want to watch the next episode in the series or a different one?' asks Willow.

'I'm happy to watch another episode or two before I decide if I really like it.'

* * *

Showered, teeth brushed, snuggled underneath the doona in Aalia's bed, Willow gazes up at the moonlit ceiling and asks, 'Do you believe in reincarnation?'

'I'm not sure. I don't think so. Do you?'

'My dad doesn't, but my mum did,' she says. 'My mum said she was more spiritual than religious. She liked the teachings of Buddha and Krishna.'

'Oh, okay. Umm, what does Buddha say about reincarnation? Is that like when you die depending on whether you were a good or bad person you can come back as another person, or an animal or even an insect? I wouldn't want to come back as an insect.'

'Most people think reincarnation is a teaching of Buddhism, but it isn't. Buddha taught about rebirth, but he meant renewing ourselves continually to improve. We're always changing.'

'So, what does Buddha say happens when you die?' Aalia asks.

'From memory, it has something to do with energy

changing to take on another form and shape. Which I guess is referring to our soul, but nothing about it re-entering another body.'

'So where did the idea of reincarnation come from?' Aalia asks, propping herself onto her side with her elbow, facing Willow.

'Hindus believes when you die your body dies but not your soul. And your soul lives in a second world in an astral body until it's reborn into a physical body back to earth. This occurs many times as your soul develops and becomes enlightened.'

'So, I guess if you lived a good life by being honest, kind and helped people, you get to come back as another human being, and maybe into a better life,' says Aalia.

'Yes, it's based on karma, all your life's actions.'

'I don't want to come back as someone else, forgetting my life, my family, and my friends.'

'I don't either. I wonder if my mum is still an astral soul out there waiting to be reborn. If it's true, will I run into her one day? Will I know it's her? Will she recognise me?' Willow sniffs, wiping tears from her cheeks with her pyjama sleeves.

Aalia places her arm around Willow, resting her head on her shoulder. 'I think your mum is in the afterlife, looking over you like a guardian angel. One day when it's your time, which won't be for a long, long time, you'll see each other again. That's what I believe. Same with my grandma and Charlotte.'

'I hope so. I like that idea. There are times I do feel my mum around me,' Willow discloses.

'That's because she is. Just like I feel that way about my grandma and Charlotte.' Hesitatingly, she asks, 'How...did your mother die?'

Willow inhales, before responding in a quiet voice. 'She died of pancreatic cancer. She was in a lot of pain.'

'Oh, I'm sorry,' Aalia murmurs.

After a long pause Willow puffs up her pillow, and says, 'Well, I'm tired. I can't wait to get up and play with Sapphire tomorrow morning. Goodnight.' Turning onto her side facing the window, with her back towards Aalia, she stares out in silence.

'Goodnight,' mumbles Aalia lying on her back staring up at the ceiling until she falls into a slumber punctuated with disturbing dreams.

* * *

While getting dressed in the morning, Aalia notices several elongated scabbed cuts on Willow's left upper thigh. Hesitantly, she asks, 'Uh, how did you manage to cut yourself? Does it hurt?'

Quickly pulling up her jeans, Willow responds dismissively, 'Oh, that's nothing. I accidently cut myself shaving in a rush.'

'Oh, okay,' Aalia responds, crinkling her forehead, narrowing her eyes.

'Let's go and see Sapphire; I heard her meowing late last night,' Willow suggests, heading towards the bedroom door.

'Sure, I guess I was tired. I didn't hear her,' admits Aalia.

'You were dead to the world. I pushed you onto your side when you started snoring and moaning,' Willow confesses, grinning.

'Sorry, about that, I must've been tired.' She opens the laundry door slowly and carefully so as to not to hit Sapphire, who's loudly mewing, reaching underneath the door with her front paws.

Chapter Eleven

'Gather in groups of three or four,' directs Mrs O'Sullivan. 'These will be your discussion groups for breakout activities, and group presentation for the remainder of the term.'

Students turn to those closest to them. Pairs of students wander up to other pairs or individuals hoping to form an alliance.

'Hi Aalia,' says Emma with a friendly smile, standing in front of her desk and looking down at her with her dark warm brown eyes. 'Maddy's sick today. I was wondering if she and I could join you and Willow?'

Simultaneously Aalia and Willow both look up at Emma, mirroring her smile and say, 'Yes, that'd be great.'

They overhear Paris coldly say, 'No, Adam our group is full.' She and her inseparable blonde sidekicks, Belle and Sophia, want to remain exclusive.

Mrs O'Sullivan encourages other pairs or groups of three to include those who do not belong to a group until all the students are absorbed, thanking them for their cooperation. She continues, 'I'd like you to break out in your groups and discuss the questions on the whiteboard. I'll give you fifteen minutes before reporting your thoughts back to the class.'

* * *

Scanning the bus for an empty seat Aalia spots Liam sitting towards the back. Their eyes meet. His face lights up and he nods, raising his eyebrows and inviting her to sit down next to him.

Placing her backpack on her lap she slides next to him. 'Hi; thanks.'

'Hey, how've you been?' he asks.

'Good. I have a new kitten... Sapphire. She's so cute. Very playful and affectionate. You should come over and meet her one day.'

'That's cool. Yeah, I will.'

'Any more signs from Charlotte, like the wind chimes?' she asks hopefully.

'No, unfortunately. The only time I feel her around is when I pray for her,' he discloses. 'I guess she's having too good of a time and is busy these days.' He smiles but there's sadness reflected in his eyes.

'I'm sure she'll visit you again or show you a sign.'

'I guess no further clues as to what Charlotte's message meant?' he asks.

Aalia pauses, before saying, 'No, not really. She's obviously grieving the way we are. She stayed over on the weekend. Actually, she came with me and Mum to the Pet Rescue when I got Sapphire.' She turns face forward feeling slightly guilty about not mentioning the cuts on Willow's thigh. She reflects; *Maybe she did cut herself shaving. Afterall, I've cut myself on many occasions when in a rush, around my ankles. Once I took a chunk out. I still have the scar.*

'Are you finding that book Mum lent you useful?' he asks.

'Yes, I am, but I haven't read much of it yet. I've had lots of homework, and I've been spending time with Willow and now Sapphire,' she admits. 'Can I ask you something?'

'Yep, can't promise I'll know the answer though.'

'Do Bahá'ís believe in reincarnation?'

'No, that's a man-made idea. Thank goodness. Can you imagine coming back here as someone else into a different family but forgetting your previous life? Or worse, coming back as an animal or insect, like a cockroach?'

'I would like to think we don't. Just wondering.' She glances at him before gazing out the window.

'There's probably something in the book that explains it in more detail. All I know is that there are an infinite number of worlds, and there's no need for us to return to this earth to develop ourselves spiritually. Continually returning sounds like hell to me,' he says.

'Yes, it would be awful,' she agrees. 'I'll have a closer look at the book.'

'Next stop is mine,' he announces.

'Oh, okay,' she says, standing up to let him out.

'It was great seeing you again.' He smiles as he brushes past her holding his backpack. 'I'll come over to see Sapphire before she gets too big.'

'Yeah, that'd be good. Bye,' she calls out as he walks towards the front of the bus.

* * *

'Hello, you,' says Aalia affectionately, gently rubbing her face against Sapphire's. 'Oh, how I've missed you. Did you miss me?' she asks, kissing the top of the kitten's head.

Sapphire's body rumbles as she purrs loudly. Aalia places her onto the floor as she bends down, peering under the lounge suite in the sunroom. She pulls out the stick with the mouse tied to the string, dangling it mid-air. She laughs in delight at Sapphire's unsuccessful attempts to catch the mouse, leaping through the air like a flying trapeze artist.

Stomach grumbling, she scoops up Sapphire, and heads to the kitchen. Standing on her tiptoes she searches the top shelf of the pantry right up the back blindly feeling with her outstretched hand. 'Where are those emergency chocolate biscuits Mum has hidden?' With no sign of any biscuits or sweets, she reluctantly grabs a pack of sea salted popcorn. She sighs. 'I bet Dad sneaked and ate those biscuits. I guess this is better than nothing.'

Eating the popcorn straight from the bag she watches TV, petting Sapphire curled up in her lap.

Eventually when Sapphire falls asleep. Aalia places her next to her onto the lounge. Recalling her earlier conversation with Liam about reincarnation she retrieves the book from her room and leafs through the pages searching for any information about reincarnation. 'Ah ha, here we go,' she says aloud and begins reading.

Moreover, this material world has not such value or such excellence that man, after having escaped from this cage, will desire a second time to fall into this snare. No, through the Eternal Bounty the worth and true ability of man becomes apparent and visible by traversing the degrees of existence, and not by returning... Besides, advancing and moving in the worlds in a direct order according to natural law is the cause of existence, and a movement contrary to the system and the law of nature is the cause of non-existence. The return of the soul after death is contrary to the natural movement and opposed to the divine system.

Therefore, by returning, it is absolutely impossible to obtain existence; it is as if man, after being freed from the womb, should return to it a second time.[5]

She closes the book, gently placing it on the coffee table as not to disturb Sapphire. Gazing out the window deep in her own thoughts she reflects; Glad to know there's no such thing as reincarnation. I'll always be me.

Chapter Twelve

Alia wakes up in the early hours from a restless sleep before falling into a deep, altered state and dreams:

I'm startled when a cat jumps onto my bed and starts rubbing and butting its head against mine, purring loudly. The moonlight reveals it's a tabby cat with golden eyes. 'Abbey? Abbey is that you?' I laugh. 'Oh, how I've missed you.'

Then her stripes gradually transform, becoming wider and darker. The hairs on my neck stand up, and I freeze, as feelings of dread and terror overwhelm me. Petrified, I turn around to observe the wooden headboard turn into a sliding door and begin to open slightly. I feel the presence of an invisible, dark spirit escape from the gap. Trying to shout, my voice comes out in a hoarse whisper, as I command, 'Leave!' Summoning up all my will power I repeatedly tell whomever or whatever it is, in a voice barely audible, 'You're not welcome here! Go back to where you came from!'

I couldn't see him physically but could see the destruction and damage as he strews, flings, and smashes my belongings. He heads down the hallway. I follow in close pursuit. 'You must leave!' I demand, growling in a low voice, desperately trying to get rid of him. Every time I lunge towards him, I feel a very strong invisible force push me backwards. Surprised at my courage, and conviction, although still in a cracked whisper I declare, 'One day I'll be stronger than you.'

In a final attempt to rid the house of him, I retrieve the softball bat from the garage, and start swinging and thrashing in the air wherever I feel his presence. I'm frustrated at my futile attempts as the air meets no resistance, and he continues to push me backwards. The battle continues and moves into the kitchen, until I hear crying coming from my bedroom.

I hastily return to my room. There's a girl in a foetal position, crying underneath my doona. Frightened, concerned, and curious I slowly remove the doona from her head. It's Charlotte! For a split second I believe and want it to be her. That is until I look into her eyes, reflecting black pools filled with despair. Her eyes are unfamiliar, disturbing, and unsettling. It's not Charlotte. It's trickery. But I wasn't fooled by the dark spirit. I knew it was really him.

Aalia sits up in bed abruptly, heart racing. Shuddering, she reaches for the lamp in panic. 'It's only a dream. It's not real,' she repeats like a mantra, shaken and trying to remember to take slow deep breaths.

Chapter Thirteen

'Mmmm, this jerk chicken is amazing!' exclaims Liam before shovelling another piece into his mouth.

'It's delicious,' agrees Mr Davis. 'Don't mind if I have another piece and some more of this hot sauce,' he announces reaching across the outdoor table for seconds.

'Thank you, I'm glad you like it,' says Dad, beaming with pride. 'This sauce is my own secret recipe. Traditionally you don't have sauce with jerk chicken. Please, help yourselves.'

'This is good,' says Aalia relaxing back into the outdoor lounge chair as she wipes her mouth.

'Save room for dessert,' says Mum. 'I've made a coconut pie, and a lime meringue pie.'

'You've spoiled us,' says Mrs Davis, spooning up some more fragrant coconut rice with pigeon peas.

'I think someone's awake,' reports Aalia, pushing her chair back as she stands up upon hearing high-pitched mewing coming from the laundry.

She returns looking down adorningly at the kitten cradled in her arms. 'This is Sapphire. Isn't she beautiful?'

'She is. Can I have a cuddle?' asks Mrs Davis. Aalia hands the kitten to her gently. The kitten starts to squirm. Mrs Davis places her down on the paving to explore.

Liam finds a stick and swishes it back and forth to gain Sapphire's attention. Her eyes widen, as she crouches ready to pounce; that is until a butterfly flies past and she pursues it instead. He laughs. 'I think someone has ADHD.'

'I'll put the kettle on,' says Mum as she starts to gather everyone's plates.

'Let me help,' offers Mr Davis, standing up and collecting the food dishes.

Facing Mrs Davis, with her elbow on the table, propping up her chin, Aalia clears her throat before asking, 'Do Bahá'ís believe in guardian angels? And if so, how do they communicate with us?'

'Those are interesting questions.' Mrs Davis exhales as she leans back into her chair. 'The Bahá'i Writings don't have much to say on these topics. They're a bit ambiguous. Maybe it's one of life's mysteries we don't truly find out the answer until we pass over to the next world.'

'Oh, okay. Well, I believe in guardian angels,' says Aalia.

'It's a lovely, and reassuring thought,' agrees Mrs Davis.

Turning to Liam, Aalia asks, 'After dessert do you want to hang out in the sunroom with Sapphire? It's easier to keep an eye on her there.'

'Sounds good,' he responds.

Moments later Liam plonks onto the three-seater lounge. Lying down, he confesses, 'I'm stuffed. I don't think I could eat another thing.'

'I'm not surprised considering how much you ate.' She grins, sitting in the adjacent single lounge chair and placing

Sapphire onto the tiled floor. 'Do you remember the time Charlotte and I froze some mud in the empty chocolate ice cream container?' she recalled.

'Yeah, that was mean. I was so looking forward to eating that ice cream after school.'

'It was Charlotte's idea. She was fed up and complained about how you used to regularly leave empty containers or at most with only a mouthful of ice cream in the freezer, as well as returning packets to the pantry with only one biscuit or worse just crumbs.' She smiled in recollection. 'I actually thought it was quite ingenious.'

'Very funny. Oh, I almost forgot. Yesterday I saw an eastern yellow robin sitting on the fence while I was playing fetch with Fudge in the yard. I wonder if Charlotte sent it as a sign.' He contemplates, looking sideways and up into space.

'Probably. I haven't had any signs recently,' she admits. 'What do you think happens when you first die? Do you think it's scary and hurts?'

'I don't think so. It may hurt at first depending on how you die, but once your soul leaves your body it won't hurt.'

A shadow comes over her face, as her eyes start to water, and in a soft voice she reflects, 'At least Charlotte died quickly.'

In silence they watch Sapphire chase the colourful plastic ball with a bell inside around the room.

The silence is broken when the sliding door opens, and their parents step inside.

* * *

Wandering into the kitchen to sneak a slice of coconut pie left from lunch, Aalia discovers her mother helping herself to a piece. 'I'll join you,' she says, holding out a small plate.

Her mother smiles and places a slice onto the plate. 'Want to eat in here or in the lounge?' she asks.

'In here if that's okay. I'd like to ask you something.' She takes a mouthful and pauses, choosing her words carefully. 'Um…I was wondering what you think happens when you die. You say things like Grandma and Grandpa are in our hearts and we have our memories.'

Holding a spoonful of pie mid-air, her mother places it back down onto her plate before responding. 'Well to be honest I'm not exactly sure. I'd like to think there's a heaven and we'll all be reunited again.'

'What's heaven like? Does everyone go there?' Aalia studies her mother's face.

'I've had different thoughts about heaven and what happens when you die since I was little. When I was younger, I had to go to Sunday school. Your grandma never accompanied me, only for special services like at Christmas and Easter. She said it would make my Nanna, your great grandmother, happy.'

'When did you stop going and how come you never sent me?'

'I stopped going when I started high school. I sometimes went to the church youth group on Friday nights,' she recollected. 'Your grandma never insisted that I send you. Your father believes everyone should decide what they believe for themselves when they're an adult.'

'Are we Christians?' Aalia asks.

'I guess you could say we are non-practising Christians,' admits Mum. 'I don't believe you need to go to church to pray to God or Jesus. Jesus is in your heart.'

'Do you believe only Christians will get into heaven?'

'I always struggled with that belief. If only the Christians are going to heaven, hell will certainly be a crowded place,' laughs Mum half-heartedly. Shaking her head she says, 'No, I don't think only the Christians will go to heaven. What about the Jews? The Muslims? The Bahá'ís? And all the other good people in the world who try to help others?'

Aalia swallows another piece of pie before asking, 'Do we go straight to heaven?'

'I'd like to think so. I've met some Christians who think your soul goes into a deep sleep until Judgement Day, when Christ returns.' Her mother takes a last bite. 'But I don't think that. There must be a symbolic meaning not literal. Otherwise, it sounds as if people will arise like zombies.'

'Yeah, I don't want to become a zombie,' shudders Aalia. After scraping up the last of the pie on her plate, she collects her mother's empty plate and cutlery and stacks them in the dishwasher. 'Thanks for the pie. I'm going to read for a while before I go to sleep.'

'Goodnight, sweet dreams,' says Mum, hugging her tightly before releasing her.

Curled up in her bed under her doona, with Chino tucked under her arm, Aalia flicks through the book. *Let's see what it says about what happens when someone dies. This looks interesting.* She reads:

At first it is very difficult to welcome death, but after attaining its new condition the soul is grateful, for it has been released from the bondage of the limited to enjoy the liberties of the unlimited. It has been freed from a world of sorrow, grief and trials to live in a world of unending bliss and joy.

The phenomenal and physical have been abandoned in order that it may attain the opportunities of the ideal and spiritual. Therefore, the souls of those who have passed away from earth and completed their span of mortal pilgrimage...have hastened to a world superior to this. They have soared away from these conditions of darkness and dim vision into the realm of light.[6]

She turns off the lamp and slides down, pulling the doona up under her chin, clasping Chino to her chest. *I wonder if Charlotte found it difficult to welcome death. Probably, it happened so quickly. She didn't get to live her life.*

She rolls over to her side hugging Chino as tears roll down onto her pillow, trying to stifle her sobs.

Chapter Fourteen

Aalia pauses momentarily, turning to glance at Willow who is hunched over assembling her diorama. She seems deep in thought, with no distinguishable expression.

A frown forms across Aalia's forehead as she narrows her eyes in concern. Staring at the diorama she tentatively asks, 'Is this how you feel most of the time about your family?'

Willow stops, and straightens her posture, taking in her artwork as if looking at it for the first time. There's a figure of a female in a foetal position suspended by wire hanging from inside the shoebox. The walls are predominantly grey, with black and red slashes of paint randomly placed on all four walls of the box. Silently she studies it. 'I guess it does,' she confesses.

Aalia murmurs, 'It looks as if you're lonely, sad and in a great deal of pain.'

'Sometimes I am. But not when I'm with you,' Willow says quietly with a twisted smile.

Aalia places her arm around Willow, laying her head on her shoulder, giving her outer arm a little squeeze.

* * *

Emma, linking arms with Maddy, approaches Aalia and Willow as they're leaving the canteen, searching for a place to sit. 'Can we join you guys for lunch?' she asks.

'Sure. Let's sit over there.' Willow points towards an empty part of the low brick wall.

'Willow, this is Maddy.' Emma introduces her friend as they walk towards the wall.

'Hi, Willow. So what do you think of Glenwood High School, so far?' asks Maddy with a friendly smile.

'So far so good. Made a good friend.' Willow nods her head in Aalia's direction. 'Anyone want a slice of pizza?' she offers. 'I think my eyes are bigger than my stomach.' She passes the large pizza box around.

'Mmm!' exclaims Emma pulling a string of melted cheese from her pizza before popping it into her mouth. 'Thank you. This is so much better than my squashed sandwich.'

'Yes, thank you,' chorus the others.

A shadow forms over the pizza box. 'Well, look what we have here. Don't mind if I have a slice of pizza,' states Paris, stretching out her hand, Before she can grab a piece, the box is snatched away out of her reach. 'Hey, I want some pizza!'

'No, way,' says Willow with a scowl, quickly closing the lid, and guarding the pizza box.

'That's very rude,' scolds Paris, standing affronted with her hands on her hips.

'You are the epitome of rudeness,' declares Willow. 'Go

and get your own lunch. You're ruining our appetites.' She smiles sweetly, blinking.

'Get stuffed,' snaps Paris. She flicks her long blonde hair over her shoulder, turns and addresses her entourage. 'Come with me. Who'd want to have lunch with these losers anyway? Certainly not me.' She marches off, with Belle and Sophia in tow.

'Talk about drama. She's so up herself!' exclaims Maddy.

They agree in unison and continue to eat their pizza, relieved that the Paris drama is over. At least for now.

* * *

'I'm so happy your parents agreed to let you come to my house after school,' puffs Willow excitedly, as they power walk up the hill and through Red Gum Park.

'Me too,' agrees Aalia.

'Here's where I live,' Willow announces, holding out her arms as they walk up a driveway towards a white two storey Queenslander with an expansive veranda, trimmed evergreen hedges and a maple tree in the centre of the front yard. She retrieves a key from under a barrel pot next to a wooden bench.

Pushing open the front door she stands aside, motioning Aalia to enter. 'Welcome to my humble abode,' she announces as she performs an exaggerated bow from the waist.

'Wow, this is a big house for two people,' Aalia says in awe, looking up at a large wooden banister to a second floor before turning to her right, taking in the large sitting room with French doors and French windows leading to the front veranda. 'It's beautiful, though.'

'Thank you. Yes, it's even bigger than our other house. I don't like being here on my own at night with all the windows and doors and the large verandas. I get a bit spooked,' Willow confesses.

'What? Why are you alone at night? Where's your dad?'

'Not all the time— just when Dad has a late business meeting or work function to go to.'

'Well, maybe sometimes you can stay with us those nights, so you won't be alone.'

'That'd be nice. I'll ask next time. Thanks.' She smiles appreciatively as she puts her school bag down next to a large hallway table. 'Let's go and see what we can find to eat,' she offers. 'I'm starving.'

'Me too.' Aalia puts her backpack next to Willow's. Her eyes bulge at the size of walk-in pantry stocked full. 'Wow, this is like a little shop or canteen of your own!' she exclaims.

'I guess my dad wants to ensure at least I won't starve to death,' Willow comments. 'There are chips, crackers, and biscuits. Or if you like, ice cream, sausage rolls, or meat pies,' she suggests, opening the large double door fridge/freezer and revealing its contents.

'What do you feel like?' Aalia asks, too overwhelmed with so many options.

'I know it's still a bit cold, but I'm craving ice cream with hot fudge sauce.' Willow smiles, holding up a container of salted caramel ice cream.

Aalia's mouth waters and she enthusiastically agrees. 'That sounds delicious. You know me. I never say no to anything with chocolate.'

'That's settled.' Willow grabs the fudge sauce out of the pantry before taking out two large bowls and a couple of dessert spoons.

'I'm in heaven,' exhales Aalia as the hot fudge sauce and salted caramel ice cream melt and merge together in her mouth.

'I know what you mean.' Willow grins, contentedly digging into her ice cream and trying to cover her spoon with as much fudge sauce as it can hold. 'Want a tour of the house and check out my bedroom?' she adds.

'Sure.' Aalia gets off the barstool, holding her bowl tightly, and licking the sauce off the spoon. She peers in each room as the doors are opened along the hallway upstairs. She asks, 'How many bathrooms do you have?'

'Three, and here's the gym room,' Willow says, walking into the middle of the room. 'I don't really use it. But my dad does. Walking to school and all those stairs at school is enough exercise for me. Sometimes I will use the treadmill and spin bike, but not often.'

'Yeah, I'm not really into the gym either.'

Closing the door behind them, Willow leads Aalia to a door at the end of the house. 'This is the best room, where I spend most of my time. Ignore the mess.' She opens the door slowly, stepping into the room. 'Well, what do you think?'

'It's great. It's so big, and bright,' Aalia says enthusiastically. She looks out one of the large windows with an expansive view of Red Gum Park and the surrounding roof tops. 'Wow, what a view. Oh, look you even have a couch to lie on to read or watch something. And your own TV! You're so lucky. My parents won't allow me to have a TV in my room.'

'Now you see why it's my favourite room.' Willow opens another door leading to an en suite. 'I have everything I need, minus a fridge.'

'Do you have to clean the house? Cleaning one

bathroom is enough for me. I couldn't imagine cleaning three every week.'

'No, we have a cleaner that comes in once a week.'

'Lucky you. I am the cleaner at home,' mumbles Aalia.

Plonking herself onto the couch, Willow asks, 'What would you like to do? Watch some anime? Or a movie? Or hang out?'

Joining her on the couch Aalia picks up a cushion, holding it at arms-length to admire the colourful beaded dragonfly on it. 'I love this cushion. It's beautiful.' She turns to Willow and notices her expression turn solemn.

'It was my mum's. She loved dragonflies.' She stares at the cushion.

Aalia softly caresses the cushion before handing it to her.

Preoccupied in her own thoughts momentarily, Willow discloses, 'Since my mum died, I often see dragonflies at times and places I don't expect to see them. I wonder if it's my mum sending me a sign to tell me she's okay.'

'Yes, it probably is.' Aalia smiles. 'I researched a few weeks ago about how our loved ones who die communicate with us. Liam, Charlotte's younger brother, and I had this amazing experience when I visited with my mum, where there was no wind but the wind chimes in their backyard started to play a melody!' She continued breathlessly, 'And at the funeral there was an eastern yellow robin sitting on the fence quietly listening to the service. It was Charlotte's favourite local bird. And even Liam mentioned when he was in the backyard playing with his dog Fudge, he saw a yellow robin sitting on the fence watching him. How cool is that?'

'That's cool,' Willow concedes.

Studying Willow's face, Aalia pauses, moving her

mouth sideways before suggesting, 'Umm, I heard there's a series we can stream about people who've had different experiences around death. They died and then they were resuscitated. And their loved ones have communicated with them from beyond the grave.'

'Oh, that sounds interesting.' Willow starts to search the internet. 'Listen to this. People often describe the colours as so bright on the other side, that our brightest fluorescent colours on Earth are muddy in comparison. They're unable to find the words to describe their experiences as the colours are so vibrant and do not exist on Earth.' She continues, 'Many NDErs describe an out of body experience looking down at their body while being able to see in all directions simultaneously.'

'What else does it say?' asks Aalia, leaning forward to have a better view of the laptop screen.

'Oh wow! They've found people who were born blind, who've had a near-death experience, and saw for the first time while in the afterlife! How cool would that be?'

'It'd be amazing, but then depressing to return to their body and be blind again,' she reflects.

'That's true, but at least when it's their time, they know they'll be able to see in the afterlife.' Willow continues reading. 'Here's another case study. A woman was rushed to the hospital suffering a massive heart attack and had to be resuscitated. She had an out of body experience in which she travelled outside the hospital and saw a sneaker on the ledge of the third storey. A researcher went to investigate and found the exact shoe which the woman had described in detail.'

'Does it say anything about reincarnation? If it's true or not?' Aalia asks.

'Hmm, let's see,' Willow says aloud as she scrolls down

before deciding it's quicker to use the search function, and types in reincarnation. 'Here we go. It says several of the Hindu ideas about the afterlife were never portrayed by Indian patients' visions following their near-death experiences. None mentioned reincarnation.'

'That's a relief to hear. It confirms what I read in the book about the afterlife Liam's mother lent me,' sighs Aalia.

'What book?'

'A Bahá'i book she gave me when I visited with my mum a few weekends ago.'

'Oh, okay. What is a Bahá'i? I've never heard of it,' Willow says.

'The Bahá'i Faith the world's youngest religion. They believe all the religions come from the same God, and about the oneness of humanity.'

'Who do they follow? What's the name of their prophet?'

'Bahá'u'llah, and it took me a while to learn to say his name properly,' Aalia admits.

'What does the book say about reincarnation?'

'Basically, it's a made-up concept. We have one soul which lives for eternity through all the different worlds of God. This world is the first of many, and we should view it like a journey,' Aalia summarises.

'I like the sound of that. What does it say about meeting your family and friends?' Willow looks wistfully into Aalia's eyes momentarily before glancing at a photo of her mother in a silver frame on a bedside table in the corner between the couch and the bedframe.

'I haven't read that far yet,' she confesses. 'When I come across it, if it's in there, I'll let you know what it says.' Deep in thought for a few seconds she breaks the silence, and asks, 'When's your dad's next meeting? I'm not allowed sleepovers on school nights, but you could come over after school and have dinner with us and your dad could pick you up afterwards.'

Willow's face lightens up. 'I'm not sure, but I'll find out. Thanks.'

They both freeze momentarily when they hear a loud knock on the front door. Aalia quickly looks at the time on her mobile. 'I can't believe it's already 5:00 pm. That'll be my mum.'

They briefly hug before heading towards the door. 'I'll ask my mum about you coming over for dinner next time your dad works late.'

Chapter Fifteen

Aalia scans through the book after dinner before doing her homework to see what she can find about seeing dead relatives in the afterlife. Her eyes are drawn to the following paragraph:

And know thou for a certainty that in the divine worlds the spiritual beloved ones will recognise one another, and will seek union with each other, but a spiritual union. Likewise, a love that one may have entertained for anyone will not be forgotten in the world of the Kingdom, nor wilt thou forget there the life that thou hadst in the material world.[7]

'I knew it,' she reaffirms aloud as a warm fuzzy feeling spreads inside. Feeling reassured she closes the book and returns it to her bedside table. She stretches, reaching for her school backpack, dragging it up onto her bed. She searches through her loose papers and notebooks for her English novel. As she's pulling it out, her mobile vibrates and then stops. Dropping the book on her lap, she quickly swipes and checks her messages.

It's a message from Liam. I wonder what he wants.

The SMS reads: 'Hi, want to be involved in a junior youth service project, painting large terracotta pots for the Glenwood Aged Care Residence?'

She texts back: 'Sounds good but need more information. Talk tomorrow on the bus. Got homework.'

Liam texts back: 'Great, chat tomorrow.'

Reminiscing, she recalls, *Charlotte wanted to start up a junior youth group, and was doing some training to become an animator.*

She puffs up her pillows, places them against the headboard and opens her novel to the folded page corner marking her place.

Struggling to concentrate, she stretches and yawns while checking the time. An hour has passed. Satisfied with her efforts she folds the corner of the page, before returning the book to her backpack.

Using her laptop, she searches for more information on near-death experiences and reads several case studies. She's particularly drawn to those involving children and young people. She sits up and leans against the headboard. *Imagine meeting a sibling you didn't even know existed in the afterlife! A sibling that was stillborn or miscarried and you didn't even know existed because your parents never told you! Hmm.*

She glances at the time and decides to sneak into the laundry to have a play and cuddle with Sapphire before going to sleep.

She slowly opens the laundry door and peers inside. Sapphire is asleep in her cat cave bed. The kitten slowly starts to stir, squinting her eyes as they adjust to the mobile phone light. She crawls out, stretching, and starts mewing. Aalia scoops her into her arms, kissing and cuddling her. The silence is soon filled with contented purring.

* * *

Aalia sits on the end of the seat, reserving a spot for Liam on the afternoon school bus.

'Hi,' he calls out, as he walks up the aisle towards the middle of the bus.

'Hey.' She scoots towards the window, curious to hear more about the service project. 'So, tell me about painting pots for the Glenwood aged care.'

His face lights up. With enthusiasm he explains, 'I'm assisting Sahana, who's an animator, with a newly formed junior youth group. We're getting a bunch of the JY to paint four large terracotta pots on the theme of unity. We'll then pot them with some nice flowers and deliver them to be placed in the Memory Garden.' He asks, 'Would you like to join us?'

'Sure. When and where?'

'Next Saturday afternoon at the Glenwood Park depending on the weather. If it rains my parents said we can use the rumpus room and garage at our house.'

'What time?'

'Three o'clock followed by a barbecue.'

'Sounds good. Can I invite a friend?' she asks.

'That'd be great. I'll send the flyer.' He relaxes into the seat.

'Do I need to bring anything for the barbecue?'

'No, not really.' Looking down bashfully, he hints, 'I'm sure everybody would love your mum's famous brownies.'

She laughs. 'Sure I'll ask Mum to make some.'

'Great. By the way who are you inviting?'

'Willow. She does Visual Arts with me.'

'Okay. Great, I'll finally get to meet her.' He hesitates, shifting in his seat, looking out the window before turning back to her. 'Aaah, have you worked out how to help her?'

'What? Oh, no. Not yet. Actually...maybe I've been doing it all along.' She sits back in her seat, staring out to space.

'What do you mean?' he asks.

'We've been chatting, and researching things about the afterlife,' she recalls. 'When you think about it, it's just her and her dad here. Her dad's always busy at work. Now she's got me to talk to about her mother's death.'

'That's true. Well, I guess time will tell.'

'Have you read much about near-death experiences?' she asks.

'No, what do you mean?'

'It's when people are clinically dead, and then resuscitated. Afterwards, they often report similar experiences all over the world. Even kids.'

'That sounds really interesting,' says Liam, nodding.

'It is. One of the case studies was a five-year-old girl who had meningitis and fell into a coma. She met a girl about ten years old who said she was her sister, and their parents had called her Rietje for short. Rietje kissed her and told her to return.' Aalia continues, 'When she returned to her body, and woke up, she recounted to her parents what happened. They were very shocked and confessed Rietje had died from poisoning. They planned on telling the girl and her siblings when they were old enough to understand.'

'That would have been an amazing experience. Imagine finding out you have even more siblings and you reunite in the afterlife!'

'Yeah, that would be a nice surprise,' she comments, frowning slightly.

The bus pulls in to the stop.

Rising to depart Liam turns, and says, 'I'm glad you're coming to the JY service project. I'm looking forward to meeting the infamous Willow.'

* * *

'Thanks for dinner,' compliments Aalia before scraping the last of the curry sauce from her plate. She puts her plate and cutlery into the dishwasher. Suddenly she remembers. 'Oh, I saw Liam on the school bus this afternoon. I agreed to get involved in a junior youth service project being held at Glenwood Park next Saturday afternoon at three o'clock.'

'That sounds nice. What sort of service project?' asks Mum.

'We're going to paint large pots, plant them out and donate them to the Memory Garden at Glenwood aged care.'

'I'll drop you off and pick you up that afternoon,' offers Dad.

'Thanks Dad. I'm going to invite Willow. Can we give her a lift?'

'Of course,' he answers.

'Also, Mum can you please make some of your brownies? There's going to be a barbeque afterwards. Liam hinted how much everyone loves your famous brownies.'

'I'd be more than happy to. Do you know how many people might be there?'

'No, but two batches will be more than enough. I'm sure Liam and I would be more than happy to have any leftovers. I'm going to take a break now before studying.' She stops, turns around, and appreciatively says, 'Thanks again for dinner and for agreeing to make brownies.' She heads to the laundry to collect Sapphire on the way to the sunroom.

'You're welcome, sweetheart,' replies Mum.

Sapphire climbs in and out of her lap, rubbing against and intermittently massaging Aalia's legs with her little paws. Petting the top of her head, smiling affectionately as the kitten purrs loudly, lapping up the attention, Aalia phones Willow.

'Hello?' she answers.

'Hey, it's me Aalia. Didn't my name come up on your screen?' she asks.

'I just automatically picked it up and didn't check to be honest. I was in the middle of my assignment. What's up?'

'You remember me mentioning Liam, Charlotte's younger brother? Well, he invited us to a junior youth service project to paint large pots next Saturday afternoon for the Memory Garden at the local aged care place. Afterwards there's a barbecue and I'm bringing Mum's yummy brownies. Do you want to come? We can pick you up and drop you off. Say, yes,' she pleads.

'I'd love to. Sounds great. What are you up to? I'm no longer in the zone for studying.'

'Not much; just playing with Sapphire and talking to you. I guess I'm procrastinating about working on my assignment. Since it's not due for a couple of weeks I'm not yet feeling stressed about it. I do better under stress sometimes or at least it motivates me,' she confesses.

'Yeah, I get that. But now that we're doing that project next Saturday and I wanted to see if we could do something together this weekend, like go to the shopping mall and maybe see a movie, I'll try to get it over and done with.'

'I'd love to go to the mall and see a movie. I'll ask my

parents later but I'm sure they'll say yes. We can check out what's on tomorrow. I know this amazing gelato place you're going to love,' Aalia says excitedly. 'Well, I'd better get into the assignment too.' She laughs slightly. 'Now I'm feeling pressured. See you tomorrow. Oh, before I go don't forget to ask your dad about the project and barbecue.'

'I won't. See you tomorrow.'

Holding Sapphire mid-air above her face she kisses her paws as the kitten gently presses onto her face. She hugs her one last time before returning her to the laundry for the night. 'Goodnight Sapphire, I have an assignment to do, and you're just too cute, and distracting,' she gushes before quietly closing the door.

Chapter Sixteen

'Wow! Look at you all dressed up!' exclaims Willow, opening the front door to let Aalia in.

Aalia has dressed in a lantern sleeve plaid tweed dress with black tights and boots to match.

Willow steps out and waves to Aalia's dad to acknowledge him before he reverses out of the driveway. 'I need to change. I look daggy compared to you. Too casual,' she insists, leading Aalia up to her bedroom.

'Where's your dad? Isn't he taking us to the mall?' asks Aalia, looking around.

'He's at the car wash. He'll be back in a few minutes.' She opens her closet and flicks through her clothes, looking for just the right outfit. She pauses and pulls out an emerald V necked knitted dress. 'Just what I was looking for,' she declares. 'Now I need to find a pair of black tights and black leather boots,' she mumbles to herself while rummaging at the bottom of her closet and then in her dresser. 'Voila, the perfect outfit!' She smiles, holding up all the items in her hands.

'That green dress will make your eyes, stand out,' says Aalia. 'Love the boots.'

'Thank you.' Willow starts stripping, peeling off her denim jeans, revealing a couple of red angry cuts across her thigh. Suddenly self-conscious, she turns away from Aalia, quickly pulling up a pair of black tights.

Tight-lipped, Aalia moves towards the window providing Willow with some privacy while gathering her thoughts. *Are those new cuts or cuts reopened? She's cutting herself again. But why?*

'How do I look?' Willow asks, twirling around modelling her outfit.

'You look great. Beautiful,' Aalia says with a twisted smile.

Beep! beep! A car motor quietly rumbling can be heard outside. Willow glances out the window. 'My dad's here. Let's go!' She grabs her black handbag.

* * *

Knock, knock! 'Can I come in?' asks Mum, standing outside Aalia's room with two mugs.

'Yes,' calls out Aalia from her bed where she's cuddling Sapphire.

'I thought this might cheer and warm you up,' Mum offers, handing Aalia a cup of hot chocolate with melted marshmallows on top. 'I even added some hazelnut syrup.'

Sitting up against the headboard, Aalia reaches for the hot chocolate. 'Thanks. Hmmm,' she says slowly drawing in a sip.

'May I join you?' Mum asks. She's gently smiling, trying to read Aalia's mood.

'Sure.' She shuffles over, creating room on her bed.

Curiously, Sapphire wanders towards Aalia's mother, climbing onto her lap and trying to peer into the mug.

Mum raises the mug slightly. 'What did you two get up to today, at the mall?'

'We mainly did some window shopping. Willow bought herself some earrings, and nail polish. We went to the movies. It wasn't as good as we thought it'd be.' She continues, 'Oh, when we were walking to the gelato place, we ran into Emma and Maddy from school. So, they came with us, and we hung out until it was time for Willow's dad to pick us up and drop me home.'

'Sounds like you had a lovely day. Sorry the movie wasn't great,' Mum responds. 'You seem a little upset, though. Is it because your father and I said you can't sleep over at Willow's? You know we don't know her father that well. We're just being protective.'

'What? No. No, I'm not upset about that. I'm not really upset about anything. Just concerned.'

'What about?' Mum queries. She turns her attention to Sapphire whose claw is stuck in her cardigan. She gently moves the claw from the woollen threads.

'I'm not sure what to do.' Aalia exhales. 'About Willow. She's hurting herself.'

'Hurting herself, how?' Mum asks, leaning forward with her forehead crinkling slightly.

'I noticed it when she slept over here. Long scabbed-over cuts on her upper thigh. She told me she cut herself shaving. Not sure how you can do that, but I let it go.' She hesitates and places her mug on the bedside table. Wringing her hands, she continues. 'But then today she changed into a dress since I was wearing one. I noticed there were new red cuts on her thigh. She quickly turned her back to me to finish getting dressed. Neither of us said anything.'

'It sounds like self-harming,' says Mum. 'I understand she'd be missing her mother and trying to cope with all the changes with the move, starting a new high school. It's not easy.'

'No, it's not. I thought she was happy though.'

'People self-harm for different reasons including when they're grieving. She needs to see a counsellor. You can't help her with this. She needs a professional,' advises Mum.

'I don't think she'll go. Her dad sent her to a counsellor after her mother died. What would I say to her?' Conflicted, she slumps. She's relieved at sharing the burden weighing her down, but a ball of anxiety grows within at the thought of confronting Willow. She places a hand over her abdomen to try and ease the pressure.

'I suggest you have a chat with the school counsellor, Mr Elliot,' urges Mum. 'Willow needs you as her friend, not her counsellor. Not with something as potentially serious as this.'

'Okay, I'll think about it.'

'Well, it's getting close to my bedtime. Goodnight,' Mum says, leaning across and hugging her tightly. 'Do you want me to put Sapphire to bed?'

'Yes, please,' murmurs Aalia.

'Love you,' Mum says, scooping up Sapphire and collecting the mugs before leaving the room.

'I love you too. Wait, let me say goodnight to Sapphire.' She climbs out of bed and kisses Sapphire on the top her head. She whispers into the kitten's ear, 'I love you too.'

* * *

Stirring in her sleep, grabbing the edges of her doona and tucking them underneath to create a cocoon, Aalia dreams:

I wake up with a sense of foreboding and dread. Peering over the doona cover pulled tightly under my chin, I watch as my walls turn into a membrane. It's as if I'm in some sort of bubble. A dark shadow swims past on the other side. I freeze. My heart pounds against my chest. I hold my breath. What's going on? What was that?

The dark shadow reappears. My eyes track the creature with long tentacles as it swims more slowly alongside the membrane. I'm unable to move as it circles.

Forced to take a breath, my eyes widen in horror as several parts of the membrane bulge inwards as the creature pushes the wall with its tentacles. I pray, 'Please God do not let it through!'

After several unsuccessful attempts the creature disappears intermittently and circles, searching for a weak point of entry. I tremble, feeling hopeless, with no escape in sight.

Aalia's eyes fly open. She scrambles to sit up in bed, back against the headboard. Pulling the doona up to cover her mouth, and breathing rapidly, she frantically scans the room. *It's a nightmare. It isn't real.* She reassures herself of this while studying her four solid walls.

Chapter Seventeen

'Willow this is Liam. Liam this is Willow,' introduces Aalia with a friendly smile.

'Hi Willow, glad you could come too,' Liam says with a genuine wide grin.

'Thanks for inviting me,' Willow says, mirroring his grin.

Looking longingly at the large plastic container in Aalia's hands, Liam asks, 'Is that your mum's famous brownies?'

'Yes. Where do I put these?'

'Over on that table under the rotunda where the Esky and water cooler are,' he indicates. 'Come and I'll introduce you to Sahana, and some of the others.'

They follow Liam towards the rotunda under which there are several picnic tables, some of which are covered in newspaper and large terracotta pots, paints, and brushes. There are a dozen other young people standing around chatting. Walking past the table set aside for food and drinks, Aalia sets the container down before greeting the others.

'Everyone,' announces Liam. 'This is Aalia and Willow.'

Sahana approaches with smiling eyes to greet them. 'Welcome, I'm glad you're here. I've heard you're both very creative,' she says. 'We'll start shortly. Help yourself to some afternoon tea.'

Several of the young people make a beeline for the brownies.

Heading to join the others for some afternoon tea, Willow quietly says out of the corner of her mouth, 'You never mentioned how tall and cute Liam is.'

Aalia's eyes widen in surprise as she snaps her neck to look directly at Willow. 'He's just a friend. I don't think of him that way. Plus, he's younger than we are.'

'Only by a year,' she says grabbing two brownies. 'These are too good to risk waiting to see if there will be any left for seconds.'

A few minutes later, Sahana gathers everyone together. 'I'd like to welcome and thank you for your support of the first service project of the Spiritual Empowerment Junior Youth Group.' She continues, 'There are four large pots. I'd like to you to form groups of three and work together to paint your pot based on the theme of unity.' She turns to Liam who takes over.

He clears his throat. 'The pots will be donated to the Glenwood Age Care Residence for their Memory Garden where residents with dementia have therapy. I have a few quotes that may inspire your artwork.' He reads them aloud:

'Ye are all leaves of one tree and the drops of one sea.'

'Ye are the fruits of one tree, and the leaves of one branch. Deal ye one with another with the utmost love and harmony, with friendliness and fellowship.'

'...become one soul and one spirit; that you may become

waves of one sea, breezes of one rose-garden, flowers of one meadow and trees of one orchard.'

'Thanks Liam,' says Sahana. 'The quotes just read are based on the concept of unity, using metaphors from nature. Please select a pot and form a group of three.'

Aalia and Willow head towards one of the assigned tables. Willow picks up the laminated card containing the quotes to spark their creative juices. A younger girl with a ponytail approaches them. 'Hi, I'm Jenna. Can I join your group?' she asks hopefully.

'Yes, please do,' says Aalia.

They introduce themselves and reread the quotes aloud.

'How about we divide the pot into three segments, and each of us paints one of the metaphors provided in the quotes,' suggests Willow.

'That's a good idea,' agrees Aalia. 'You mean one of us paints the ocean, another a flower garden and someone a tree or an orchard?'

'Yes, something like that,' says Willow.

'I like that idea,' says Jenna. 'Can I paint the ocean scene?'

'Yep, I was thinking of painting a tree, symbolising the tree of life,' says Willow.

'Okay, that sounds good. I'll do a meadow with lots of colourful flowers,' decides Aalia.

Time passes quickly. The girls occasionally chat and stop to comment on each other's work but otherwise they work in silence, engrossed in their painting.

Sahana circle the groups to chat, checking each group's progress. She approaches their table. 'I love your design! Liam was right; you're very creative,' she says enthusiastically. 'It looks nearly done. Some of the others have just finished and are hanging out while the kebabs are cooked. Join us when you're ready.' she wanders off to join the others engaged in a game of soccer.

At the end of the barbecue, Aalia, and Willow approach Sahana and Liam.

'Thanks for inviting us. We had a really good time,' says Aalia.

'Yeah, thanks. I enjoyed myself. I especially loved those kebabs,' confesses Willow, grinning and placing a hand on her abdomen.

'I'm glad you were able to come,' says Sahana. 'I know you're the older ones here today. The others are around eleven to twelve. But if you're interested, I wouldn't mind starting a youth group with you guys, and Liam, and anyone else around your age keen to join,' she offers.

'I'd be,' expresses Willow, smiling keenly at Liam.

'Okay, I'll come and see what it's like first before committing,' says Aalia.

'I understand. I'll be in touch soon,' says Sahana.

'There's my dad, so we better go. Thanks again.' Aalia collects her empty container. She calls out, 'Bye Liam, see you later.'

'Bye Liam, great meeting you,' calls out Willow, jogging to catch up with Aalia who is heading towards her father's car.

Chapter Eighteen

Aalia nervously looks around to make sure no one sees her standing outside Mr Elliot's door. She inhales deeply, hesitating while holding her hand mid-air, willing it to knock against the door. Weakly, she knocks twice. Her hand drops to her side. Slightly relieved she turns around to walk away.

At least I tried.

The door abruptly swings open. Mr Elliot stands in the doorway. He smiles warmly and motions for her to enter. 'I'm sorry. I was on the phone. Please come in,' he invites.

She trudges into the office and perches on the edge of an armchair adjacent to Mr Elliott. Her eyes are downcast, and she twists her fingers as she questions her actions.

Why did I listen to Mum? I shouldn't have come.

'Would you like a drink?' he offers.

'No, thank you,' she replies, looking up briefly.

'How about a chocolate or two?' he suggests, holding up a lolly jar filled with a variety of mini chocolate bars.

'Maybe later,' she murmurs.

'Okay. Well, I'll start by reassuring you. As a counsellor I'm bound by rules of confidentiality. Whatever you tell me stays in this room. The only time I can't keep things confidential is when I'm worried about your safety or someone else's.' He continues, 'I may then have to let your family or others know so they can also help keep you or someone else safe. Your safety is my priority.' He smiles.

She briefly glances up, nodding before looking down at her hands.

'How can I help?' he asks.

'I'm not sure,' mumbles Aalia. Her tongue feels like sandpaper, as she tries to swallow. She reaches for the jug and pours herself a glass of water. She slowly takes a sip, gazing out the window at the small courtyard garden.

'What worries or issues brought you here today?' he asks.

She sighs heavily, as her shoulders drop. 'I'm worried about a friend,' she confesses.

'What's worrying you?'

'I think she's cutting herself. The first time I saw the scabbed cuts across her thigh, she told me she cut herself shaving,' unburdens Aalia.

'Sounds like maybe self-harming,' he suggests.

'Yeah, that's what my mum said, and I've been worried about it,' she admits.

'Who's the friend you're worried about?' I need to know to be able to assist.'

'Willow Hughes,' she confides.

'You mentioned the first time. Have you noticed other times she may have been self-harming?' he probes.

'Yes, a couple of weekends ago when she was getting changed before we went to the mall, I saw a couple more red, raw looking cuts. When she noticed I was looking at them, she turned her back to me.'

He reassures her, saying, 'You've done the right thing, sharing your concerns about Willow. It shows you care.'

'I do. I know she's grieving about her mum dying.' Her vision starts to blur as tears pool. 'I'm worried she wants to join her,' sniffles Aalia.

Mr Elliot places a box of tissues on the adjoining side table.

She pulls out a couple and dabs her eyes.

'I know it's been difficult losing your friend Charlotte. People experience grief differently, and sometimes it causes them to harm themselves when they're overwhelmed,' he explains. 'It sounds as if Willow needs help to work through her grief without hurting herself. I will need to talk with her.'

She straightens, slightly panicked, and tightens her lips. 'But...but she'll know it's me who told you,' Aalia stammers.

'I won't mention your name. I'll say a concerned friend,' he reassures her. 'Thank you so much for telling me. It's very courageous of you. You're a good friend. I'll check up on you in a couple of weeks or so, to see how you are,' he says.

'Oh, okay,' responds Aalia, standing up.

'You sure you don't want a couple of chocolates before you go?' he entices her.

Hesitatingly, she removes two of her favourites from the jar. 'Thank you,' she says in a lowered voice before leaving the office.

* * *

'

'How could you?' screams Willow, her face twisted in anger. Fuming, eyes blazing, she storms off out the school yard.

Aalia ashen-faced, fights back tears as she quickly glances to the gawking onlookers as they point and whisper. Humiliated, hurt, head hung low, she drags herself to the school bus.

Stone-faced she looks out the window. *I shouldn't have told Mr Elliot. Now she'll never forgive me. I've lost another best friend.* She quickly dabs the inside corners of her eyes. *Hold it together until you get home.*

The seat sags and then springs up. Liam gently places a hand on her shoulder before removing it. 'Aalia are you okay?'

'No. No, I'm not,' she confesses in a wavering voice.

'Do you want to talk?'

'Not really. Not now.'

'Okay.' He sits in silence for the remainder of the bus ride.

'Bye Aalia,' he says, as he rises to get off.

'Bye,' she mumbles, with downcast eyes as she briefly turns to acknowledge his departure.

Fumbling through blurred vision she manages to open the front door. She throws her backpack down, flings off her shoes, and runs to the laundry to retrieve Sapphire. Tears stream down her face as she lies on her bed stroking the kitten's soft coat. She cuddles and nuzzles her. 'At least you love me,' she consoles herself.

She retrieves her mobile phone from her skirt pocket, and glances at the screen. No messages. Not a word from Willow.

Depressed, she lies on her side looking out the window and absentmindedly petting Sapphire as the kitten nudges her face.

* * *

'Aalia,' calls out Mum, tapping on the door. 'Aalia, can I come in?'

She stirs, disturbing Sapphire who is snuggled against her chest. Rubbing her eyes, she looks around and notices the light's fading outside. *What time is it?*

'Are you okay?' Mum asks in concern.

'Come in,' Aalia replies. She sits up, flattens her hair and straightened her school uniform. 'I must have fallen asleep.'

Noticing her red swollen eyes, her mother looks at her tentatively. 'Do you feel okay? Are you sick or has something upset you?'

'No, I'm not sick.' Her voice cracks and the tears start to flow. 'Willow hates me! She'll never talk to me again,' she sobs, shaking.

Her mother sits on the bed holding Aalia tightly as she runs her hand over her hair. 'What happened?'

'I shouldn't have listened to you,' she cries. 'She's mad because I told Mr. Elliot. He called her into his office today. I was only trying to help but look what happened.'

'She's upset for now, but she'll calm down,' reassures Mum. 'I'm sure when she does, you'll be friends again. She'll see you were only trying to help.'

Aalia pulls away, looking her mother directly in the eyes. 'You don't know that. What if she doesn't? What if I've lost another friend?'

Mum smiles. 'You haven't lost her as a friend. Give it time,' she comforts, pulling Aalia back into her arms.

Her mother rubs her arms and kisses her gently on top of her head before standing up. 'I think Sapphire's hungry. I'll feed her. How about I order some pizza for dinner?' she suggests.

'I'm not really hungry,' Aalia murmurs.

'I'll order your favourite and request extra cheese,' Mum tempts before exiting with Sapphire, closing the door softly behind her.

Aalia types a text to Willow. 'I'm so sorry. I just wanted to help. Please forgive me.'

She stares in anticipation at the screen. Three dots appear, then disappear.

* * *

Later that evening she quietly calls out from her bed, hugging Chino, 'I need your help, Charlotte. I tried to help Willow, but I'm afraid I've made things worse.' She scans the room, looking desperately for any signs.

She reaches for the book about how the departed communicate with someone still on earth. She reads:

A conversation can be held, but not as our conversation. There is no doubt that the forces of the higher worlds interplay with the forces of this plane. The heart of man is open to inspiration; this is spiritual communication. As in a dream one talks with a friend while the mouth is silent, so is it in the conversation of the spirit.[8]

. . .

She closes the book, reflecting. *I need to keep my heart open for inspiration.*

Exhausted, she closes her eyes. Catching the sweet perfume of jasmine lingering in the air, she drifts in and out of sleep.

Chapter Nineteen

Staring up at the ceiling Aalia analyses her dream.

She rolls up one of her pyjama sleeves, stretching and pulling her skin with her fingers, searching for any bite marks. Her skin is smooth and unblemished. She laughs at herself. *It was only a dream. But that voice...sounded familiar. Grandma was that you? I thought I smelled jasmine last night.*

She jumps out of bed, hastily heads to the window, searching the garden and neighbours' hedges. *There's no jasmine growing outside. I don't think it's even in bloom yet.*

'That was you, wasn't it Grandma?' she asks aloud, smiling. She feels a vibrating warmth bubbling within. Tears of happiness form in her eyes.

I did the right thing. Mr Elliot said it was very courageous. Grandma confirmed that the answers are inside me. I did what was right.

As quickly as her happiness arises, it disappears as she prepares to get ready for school.

She trudges towards the kitchen, where she plops down on a kitchen stool, hugging her abdomen as she rocks slowly back and forth. 'Mum, I don't feel so well. Do I have to go to school?'

Her mother places a hand on her forehead. 'You don't have a fever. What are your symptoms?'

'I have a stomach ache.'

'Could it be you're feeling anxious about seeing Willow at school today?'

'Maybe,' Aalia confesses. 'Can I stay home, just for today? Please?'

'You're going to have to face her. It might as well be today. I know it's hard,' empathises Mum.

Aalia gives a defeated sigh. 'I can't eat breakfast. I don't think I can keep anything down.' She collects her lunch box and places it in her backpack.

'At least try to have a piece of fruit or even a piece of toast. You'll need it to keep your strength up,' Mum says. She holds out the fruit bowl.

Selecting a mandarin, Aalia mumbles, 'I'll try to eat it.'

* * *

Dread fills her as she approaches the school gates. No sign of Willow. She heads to English.

Heart thumping out of her chest, she enters the classroom with downcast eyes, and briefly glances towards her usual seat next to Willow.

Maddy and Emma are seated next her. All the seats nearby are taken. She scans the room and locates a spare seat up towards the back, right behind Paris and her peeps.

She sighs, putting her bag on the desk, and pulling the chair out before sliding in.

Paris turns and watches on with curious delight, smirking as one eyebrow lifted. She nudges her friends.

Taunting Aalia, she asks, 'Where are your friends?' She laughs. 'Oh, that's right, you don't have any.'

Ignoring her, Aalia rummages through her bag to locate her notebook, novel, and pencil case.

'Seriously, did Willow finally work out you're a loser?' Paris jeers.

Aalia feels heat radiate from her face, but she remains expressionless, not willing to provide Paris with any attention or ammunition.

She looks up in relief as Mrs O'Sullivan enters the room.

Paris stares at Aalia before turning around.

'Good morning, everyone,' Mrs O'Sullivan greets the class cheerily. 'I'm assuming you've read chapter twelve for homework. The story has taken a surprise turn.' She continues, 'Please break up into your assigned groups to discuss the questions on the whiteboard before sharing with the class your thoughts and insights. You have fifteen minutes.'

Paris whiplashes around and smiles at Aalia. 'Seems you're not wanted in your group. You can't join our group. We're full. Nobody wants you. Too bad, so sad,' she jibes.

'Get a life,' commands Aalia as she grabs her novel and heads towards her group.

'Morning,' she says hesitantly, pulling a chair from nearby and joining the group.

'Hi,' replies Emma awkwardly, looking between Willow and Aalia.

'Hey,' responds Maddy.

Willow doesn't acknowledge Aalia.

After an uncomfortable pause, Emma leads the discussion. 'I didn't expect that twist. Did you?'

'It was such a shock. I wonder what she'll do now?' asks Maddy.

The next fifteen minutes drag on as Aalia participates with minimal responses. Relief washes over her when she returns to her desk, despite Paris' penetrating stare.

She quickly shoves her belongings into her bag before heading towards the library for solace following the bell.

* * *

Absentmindedly she moves towards the window when she gets on the bus.

Liam greets her.

'Hi,' she murmurs, glancing at him before looking out the window.

'I'm glad it's the school holidays next week. Do you have any plans?' he asks.

She glances at him again before replying. 'No.'

'If you're interested, we're having a social youth gathering next Saturday night at my place. We'll be eating pizza and playing some games to see who would like to get together more regularly.' He continues, 'Sometimes we'll have short discussions on current issues like climate change, and racism and we'll plan service projects.'

'I might come. I'll let you know closer to the time if that's okay.'

'Okay. I think you'll enjoy yourself,' he encourages. 'By the way can you ask Willow? She seemed keen to join when it was mentioned at the JY service project.'

'Uh, she isn't talking to me,' she quietly admits.

'Oh, I know you were upset last week, but I didn't know why. Is that why? Have you had a fight?'

'Something like that.' She adds, 'I will send her a text

about it later next week to see if she'd be interested. Maybe it'll be a way to break the ice.'

'That sounds like a good idea. I'm sure she'll get over whatever she's mad about.'

Respecting her solemn mood, he turns, facing forward for the remainder of the bus trip.

Standing up he smiles and offers, 'Let me know if you'd like to come to the youth gathering. Or anytime during the school holidays to hang out or go and see a movie.'

'Thanks.' She smiles briefly, looking up at him before he turns to disembark.

* * *

The smell of fried chicken wafts in under the bedroom door. Aalia closes her book unable to concentrate further on her maths as her stomach starts growling. She enters the kitchen, with her mouth watering. 'Hi, that smells delicious. When will dinner be ready?'

'About half an hour. How was school?' mum asks, peeling a potato.

With a long exhale, Aalia confesses, 'Not great.' She picks up Sapphire who's rubbing against her leg, meowing. She pets her kitten distractedly.

'Oh. I guess Willow's still not talking to you.' Mum looks up briefly before adding the potatoes to the boiling pot.

'Nope. Maybe she never will,' Aalia says in a deflated voice.

'Give her time. She's hurting.'

'I can't wait for the school holidays. Oh, before I forget, Liam invited me to a social youth gathering next Saturday night at his parents' place. Not sure if I want to go or not.'

'Sounds like fun. Maybe a chance to make some new friends,' comments Mum.

'I guess so. I'll see how I feel closer to the time.' She glances at the boiling potatoes, and asks hopefully, 'Mashed potatoes?'

'Yes, with baby peas, and gravy.'

'Can't wait for dinner. I think Sapphire is hoping she's going to get some fried chicken. I'll go and feed her.'

Chapter Twenty

With a nervous intake of breath, head down, with tense and rounded shoulders Aalia enters the classroom. Uncomfortably, she sits in an empty seat towards the back. She observes the back of Willow's head as she turns to face Renae, another Visual Arts student, laughing after she whispered into her ear. Aalia's ears and cheeks burn. Relieved it's a theory lesson she takes out her notebook and sits facing the whiteboard in preparation.

She glances several times at the large ticking clock on the wall. Time drags. She ignores the occasional curious glances of the other students fliting between her and Willow.

Packing her bag upon hearing the bell, she remains seated until Willow and the other students file out.

She traipses to the bus.

As she walks up the aisle, she's relieved to see Liam already seated with a friend and engaged in conversation. Their eyes meet briefly as he nods an acknowledgment to her, while simultaneously listening to his animated friend.

She slides into a seat farther up the aisle towards the window and becomes lost in her thoughts.

* * *

Flicking between channels, Aalia pauses when she stumbles across a scene of a group of kids tackling a rope course in the treetops. She turns off the TV, and puts down the remote next to her as she's transported to a memory:

'I can't do this,' I whined, trembling, fumbling to clip on my helmet.

The outdoor adventure guide at our Year 6 camp signalled for me to proceed.

'Yes, you can,' encouraged Charlotte. 'You've got this.'

Looking down anxiously from the rainforest treetops I insisted, 'No, I don't. You go without me.'

'No, I won't. I'll be right behind you.'

'My legs are wobbling. You know I don't like heights,' I complained.

'Be brave. You have a harness and are connected to the safety line. You can't fall and hurt yourself.'

'Why did I let you talk me into this?' I deeply exhaled. Gripping the side ropes, I take a small step forward onto the rope bridge

'See, you can do it! Keep moving forward one step at a time,' cheered Charlotte.

I gradually pick up an unsteady pace. 'Yes, I can,' I said breathlessly, feeling my confidence build.

Chapter Twenty-One

S he stretches, accidently knocking Chino to the floor. She leans over to pick him up, enjoying the warmth of the sunbeam across her bed. She smiles to herself. *I can sleep in. It's the school holidays. I have the house to myself.*

In her pyjamas she wanders to the laundry. Carefully opening the door, she greets Sapphire. 'Good morning, beautiful!' She picks her up for a cuddle, before releasing the squirming kitten.

After feeding Sapphire, she wanders into the kitchen, opening the fridge and cupboards searching for something to eat. 'What do I feel like?' A pancake mix catches her eye. Holding the box, she continues searching. 'Chocolate chips!' she exclaims with happiness. 'Best breakfast ever.'

She chats to Sapphire who's exploring the kitchen while she mixes the batter. 'What will we do today? We can go out in the garden. We can watch a movie. We can paint.'

'Mmm, these are good. I've outdone myself, Sapphire,' she proudly announces and takes another huge bite.

Flicking through the channels looking for something

interesting to watch in the sunroom, she complains, 'Just news, morning shows, and kids' shows. Let's look on the internet.'

Sapphire jumps up on the lounge, and climbs onto Aalia's lap, purring loudly.

Maybe I'll watch some more of this anime series Willow loves so much.

After a couple of episodes, she retrieves her mobile phone from her room, just in case Willow or her mother sent a message. She notices one unread message. It's from her mother.

It reads: Morning, do not stay in your pyjamas all day. Please hang load of clothes. XX Mum

While hanging the laundry outside she tunes into the drone of bees sweeping back and forth over a colourful display of blooming flowers. Amused, she watches Sapphire unsuccessfully pursuing butterflies. Something metallic blue hovering above catches her eye. *A dragonfly. I wonder what Willow's doing these holidays.*

She watched the dragonfly home in on a lavender bush. Breaking off a sprig, she inhales the sweet smell. A memory's triggered:

I was sitting here in the garden with Grandma while she was snipping a basketful of lavender sprigs to make some essential oil. I asked, 'Grandma, do you ever get lonely without Grandpa?'

She stood up, paused, and then turned to me and said, 'I'm never alone. No one is. I have a couple of guardian angels, and one of them is your grandpa.' Her face radiated happiness. Her eyes shone with a look of knowing.

'Do I have guardian angels?'

She laughed heartily. 'Yes, sweetheart you do. Sometimes if you're real quiet and go within you may hear, feel, or see

one of them. Maybe even dream of them. Listen with your heart.'

'How do they help?'

'They send signs; confirmations when you're on the right path or do the right thing. The important thing is to listen to your heart and to take the first step.'

'Do some people never meet their guardian angel?' I asked.

'Some don't in this life. But just because they can't see them or don't believe in them it doesn't mean they don't exist.'

'I hope my guardian angel sends me signs. I'll try to listen more with my heart.'

Smiling to herself savouring the fond memory of her grandma, Aalia suddenly feels inspired to paint in the garden. She collects her painting supplies and her visual art diary, setting them on the outdoor table. Staring out into the garden looking for inspiration she wonders. What shall I paint? Flowers? Sapphire? The dragonfly? She starts sketching a dragonfly.

Putting the final touches on her artwork with her acrylic paints, she studies her piece. Not bad. Maybe one day I'll give it to Willow.

Stomach rumbling, she heads to the kitchen.

* * *

Later in the week, feeling bored, Aalia summons up the courage to send a SMS to Willow. She texts: 'Hi, how are you? I miss you. I'm truly sorry.'

Three dots start blinking. The reply reads: 'I'm okay. I miss you too.'

Surprised and excited, Aalia sits upright, restraining

herself from calling her immediately. She types: 'Want to go to a youth gathering at Liam's house on Saturday night for a pizza night and games?'

The reply reads: 'Sounds good. I'd love to. What time? Address?'

Aalia, dizzy from happiness, types: 'I'll find out and let you know. What are you doing tomorrow? Want to come over?'

Her mobile starts vibrating. She almost drops it in disbelief. Anxiety mixed with joy swirls, forming a bundle in her stomach. Hesitantly she answers, 'Hi.'

'Hi, thought it was easier to ring instead of texting,' says Willow.

'Yes, it is. What've you been up to?'

'Oh, nothing much. I went to the mall with Emma and Maddy on Tuesday and had lunch. Other than that, I've been just watching anime, reading, and painting.'

'Me too. I watched a few more episodes of that anime series you recommended. I'm getting into it,' Aalia confesses.

'What time did you want me to come over?' Willow asks.

'How about eleven?'

'Okay, thanks. I'll see you tomorrow.'

'Great, I can't wait. Bye.' Grinning, she absentmindedly picks up Chino and strokes him as the recent conversation loops in her mind.

* * *

'Guess what?' she ecstatically asks her mother, with a broad smile as she walks in from work. 'Willow is coming over tomorrow!'

'That's wonderful,' says Mum.

'Yes, and I know, you said she'd come around. You were right.'

'What time is she coming over? Should we pop out to the shops and pick up anything for lunch or special treats?' offers Mum.

'No, that's okay. We can make tacos and bake something ourselves.'

'Great. Now to think about what we will have for dinner. Any ideas?' asks Mum as they walk into the kitchen.

* * *

Later that evening Aalia texts Liam. It reads: 'What time is the youth gathering on Saturday? Do I bring anything? Willow's coming.'

The screen lights up. He replies: 'Great. 6pm. Wouldn't say no to brownies. ☺. Happy Willow's coming.'

Chapter Twenty-Two

Three months have passed.

'Hi, I'm home,' announces Aalia, entering the lounge room. She plonks next to her parents on the couch.

'How was the movie?' asks Mum.

'It was better than I thought it'd be. Sometime sequels aren't as good as the first. It was packed. I'm glad we got there earlier to get our tickets before eating.'

'What'd you eat?' asks Dad.

'The usual. Sushi. Liam and the others had kebabs.' Glancing at the TV, she asks, 'What are you watching?'

'A romantic comedy. Your mother's choice.' Dad looks up at the ceiling.

Mum playfully taps him on the arm.

Aalia glances down, retrieving her vibrating mobile from her pocket. She quickly swipes and answers. 'Hey, what are you up to?' She stands up to leave the room, and mouths 'Willow,' silently to her parents before heading to her room.

'I have a surprise! Can you come over tomorrow morning?' asks Willow.

'What surprise?' she asks.

'If I told you, it wouldn't be a surprise. Just go and ask your parents,' she urges.

'Not even a hint?'

'Nope.'

'Okay. What time?'

'Ten. My dad can drop you back home after lunch.'

Walking back towards the lounge, Aalia pops her head through the doorway, holding her mobile down by her side. 'Mum, Dad, Willow wants to know if you can drop me off tomorrow morning to her place. She has a surprise.' She continues, 'Her dad will drop me home after lunch. Can I go please?' She brings her hands together as if begging.

Her parents look at one another. Her father shrugs. 'Yes. What time?' asks Mum.

'Ten, she said. Thanks.' She grins before retreating to her room.

'So...how was the movie? Or more importantly Liam?' Willow continues as Aalia raises the phone again.

'The movie was good. For the millionth time, Liam's only a friend. He's like a brother to me. Plus, we went with some of the others from the youth group.'

'Anyhoo, I can't wait to show you my surprise tomorrow. All I'll say is that it's an early birthday present.'

'Sounds exciting. I can't wait,' confesses Aalia.

'Yes, believe me it is. Got to go. I'll see you tomorrow.'

The call disconnects just as the words, 'Bye,' are uttered.

* * *

'Thanks Dad,' says Aalia, getting out of the car.

'You're welcome. Say hello to Willow and her father for me.'

'I will.' She smiles as she closes the car door.

Even before she reaches the house door, it swings open and Willow steps out with a broad smile, beaming with happiness, holding a large fluffy tan, black and white puppy.

'Oh, she's so beautiful!' exclaims Aalia running her fingers through the puppy's soft fluffy coat. 'Or he?'

'Her name is Nutmeg,' gushes Willow, carrying her inside, and closing the door behind them. 'She's a rough collie. Isn't she just adorable?'

'She is. Can I have a hold?'

'Let's sit outside the back,' Willow suggests as they walk through the kitchen where Mr Hughes is reading the newspaper and drinking a cup of coffee.

He looks up, smiling, and greets Aalia. 'Good morning. Willow has been dying to show you Nutmeg.'

'I can see why; she's so beautiful. Oh, by the way my dad said to say hello.'

'We're going to play with Nutmeg out the back,' says Willow, opening the sliding door onto the back deck.

'How old is she? Where did you get her?' Aalia asks.

'She's nine weeks old. My dad had put our name down with a breeder on the Sunshine Coast a few months ago.'

'I love her name,' says Aalia, playing tug of war using a stuffed toy rabbit with the puppy.

'I just thought she looked like a Nutmeg from the moment I saw her. There were three puppies I could choose from. She was the cutest.'

'Where does she sleep?'

'I have set up a puppy play pen in my room. I put a

couple of puppy pee training pad inside on the floor of the pen until she's toilet trained.'

'You're lucky she gets to sleep in your room.'

'It'll be good when she's settled. It was hard ignoring her whining last night.' She yawns. 'When she's older I'll replace the pen with a dog bed.'

'That's one of the reasons we put Sapphire in the laundry at night. Cats, unlike dogs, are nocturnal.'

'My dad has agreed to enrol her into puppy pre-school classes run at the vet's place. He's going to come with me to learn.' Willow has a shine in her eyes.

'I think she's tired herself out,' says Aalia, laughing, as Nutmeg flops to the ground, putting her head on her paws.

Picking the puppy up gently, Willow says, 'I'll put her to sleep in her pen. After that we can grab some morning tea. We have some chocolate éclairs from the French bakery.'

'Mmm, these chocolate éclairs are heaven,' says Aalia, momentarily closing her eyes.

'They're pretty tasty,' agrees Willow.

As they sit in silence enjoying their éclairs on the outdoor hanging swing chairs, they observe flittering butterflies, listening to the backdrop of bees droning, and flies buzzing.

Willow clears her throat. Gazing down at her hands, she takes in a deep breath, which she exhales before saying, 'Thank you for being a true friend. It took a lot of courage for you to see Mr Elliot last term. I was horrible to you afterwards.'

Aalia pauses, holding her éclair midway in the air before placing it back onto her plate. She replies, 'That's okay. You were so angry; I was afraid you'd never talk to me again.'

'I was angry, wasn't I? But I needed help. Mr Elliot spoke to my dad, and they organised for me to see a doctor.' She continues, 'I'm currently on anti-depressants. I started seeing a psychologist. I still do. She's really helping.'

Smiling gently, Aalia replies, 'I'm glad. I know it hasn't been easy for you.'

'No, but you get me. You know what it's like to lose someone.'

Chapter Twenty-Three

Alia, wearing a bright yellow dress, accompanied by her parents, and carrying a bouquet of sunflowers, enters through the open front door into Mr and Mrs Davis' lounge room. It's packed with family and friends. She hands the flowers to Mrs Davis before hugging her.

Sitting reverently, she listens as prayers and readings about the afterlife are read. It seems surreal that only a year ago she was attending Charlotte's funeral. She smiles through misty eyes at Liam when their eyes meet. She then turns, glancing out the window. There's no sign of the eastern yellow robin.

She feels Charlotte's presence fill the room. *I miss you. I look forward to when we are together again.*

The memorial program ends with the following quote being read:

The nature of the soul after death can never be described, nor is it meet and permissible to reveal its whole character to the eyes of men. The Prophets and Messengers of God have been sent down for the sole purpose of guiding mankind to the straight Path of Truth. The purpose underlying Their revelation hath been to educate all men, that they may, at the hour of death, ascend, in the utmost purity and sanctity and with absolute detachment, to the throne of the Most High. The light which these souls radiate is responsible for the progress of the world and the advancement of its peoples...All things must needs have a cause, a motive power, an animating principle. These souls and symbols of detachment have provided, and will continue to provide, the supreme moving impulse in the world of being.[9]

Bibliography

Burke, John. *Imagine Heaven: Near-Death Experiences, God's Promises, and The Exhilarating Future That Awaits You.* Baker Books, Grand Rapids, Michigan, 2015.

Hayes, G. Terrill, Fisher, J. Betty, Hill, A. Richard, and Cassiday, J. Terry. *Life Death and Immortality: The Journey of the Soul.* Baha'i Publishing Trust, Wilmette, Illinois, 1994.

Long, Jeffrey, M.D. and Perry, Paul. *Evidence of the Afterlife: The Science of Near-Death Experiences.* Harper One, New York, New York, 2010.

Strobel, Lee. *The Case For Heaven: A Journalist Investigates Evidence for Life After Death.* Zondervan Books, Grand Rapids, Michigan, 2021.

References

1. 'Abdu'l-Bahá, *Some Answered Questions*. Bahá'í Publishing Trust, Wilmette, IL, 1994, pp. 227-29.
2. 'Abdu'l-Bahá, *Bahá'í Prayers*. Bahá'í Publishing Trust, Wilmette, IL, 1991, pp. 154-55.
3. Bahá'u'lláh, *Gleanings from The Writings of Bahá'u'lláh*. Bahá'í Publishing Trust, Wilmette, IL, 1990, p. 329.
4. 'Abdu'l-Bahá, *'Abdu'l-Bahá in London*. Bahá'í Publishing Trust, London, England, 1982, pp. 95-96.
5. 'Abdu'l-Bahá, *Some Answered Questions*. Bahá'í Publishing Trust, Wilmette, IL, 1994, pp. 282-89.
6. 'Abdu'l-Bahá, *The Promulgation of Universal Peace*. Bahá'í Publishing Trust, Wilmette, IL, 1982, pp. 27-48.
7. 'Abdu'l-Bahá quoted in J.E. Esslemont, *Bahá'u'lláh and The New Era*. US Bahá'í Publishing Trust, Wilmette, IL,1980, p. 190.
8. 'Abdu'l-Bahá, *Paris Talks*. Bahá'í Publishing Trust, London, England, 1972, p. 179.
9. Bahá'u'lláh, *Gleanings from The Writings of Bahá'u'lláh*. Bahá'í Publishing Trust, Wilmette, IL, 1990, pp. 156-57.